Also by Terry Grimwood

Interference
The Last Star

TOR

TERRY GRIMWOOD

Elsewhen Press

Tor
First published in Great Britain by Elsewhen Press, 2025
An imprint of Alnpete Limited

Elsewhen Press, PO Box 757, Dartford, Kent DA2 7TQ
www.elsewhen.press
British Library Cataloguing in Publication Data.
A catalogue record for this book is available from the British Library.
ISBN 978-1-915304-68-1 Print edition
ISBN 978-1-915304-78-0 eBook edition

Designed and formatted by Elsewhen Press

For Ben, Andy, Richard, Phil and Simon
– my buddies in The Ripsaw Blues Band

BEFORE

Secretary for Interplanetary Affairs, Tor Danielson was sent to the planet Ia in response to the Iaens' request for human military aid against an invader named the Tal. The Iaens were humankind's allies and the race who helped them achieve interstellar travel. They also sponsored humankind's membership of the Alliance of Planets. Tor held the deciding vote on whether Earth should contravene an Alliance directive forbidding interference in the affairs of other worlds.

Tor was a troubled man. His daughter Eva was dying and an affair with a journalist named Katherina Molale had broken his marriage. The relationship might be over, but Katherina was part of the Ia mission, as a member of the journo pack.

During the negotiations, the Iaens offered humankind a gift that will change them forever. As a demonstration of this gift, they killed Tor's advisor, Shu Qingchun, then restored him to life. This gift of resurrection would be given to humankind if they allied themselves with the Iaens to defeat the Tal. The prospect of restoring his daughter to health threw Tor into a fierce moral dilemma. The dilemma was further exacerbated by his suspicion that the World Council knew of the Gift in advance and was using his emotional turmoil as leverage to get him to vote for war and earn humankind immortality.

Katherina, meanwhile, broke free of the guards placed on the journo pack and discovered that humankind already had a military presence on Ia and was waging war against the Tal. She also discovered that the Tal were the original natives of the planet and that it was the Iaens who were the invader and aggressor.

Following an ambush, seemingly set up by Shu Qingchun, Tor found himself on the battlefield with Katherina who revealed the true situation to him. However, when rescued by a marine unit, Tor's resolve broke down. The imminent death of his daughter and the possibility of her cure using the Iaen gift was too great a temptation to resist and in a moment of weakness he ordered a tight nuke strike against the Tal. Katherina had returned to the Tal city and was killed.

PROLOGUE

Another shell slammed into the track that ran through the centre of the town. The fiery, brutal force of the blast hurled a slab of sandstone skywards and shattered it into a brief hurricane of grit that lashed at Tor Danielson's eyes and peppered the already grazed and bruised skin of his face. His ears rang, all sound was muffled, and not for the first time that day. The shockwave caused him to stagger backwards, but he remained upright and managed to hold on to the handles of the stretcher he shared with Rowland.

"Fuckers," she shouted from behind him, her voice distorted in Tor's hearing by the aftermath of the explosion. "Can't they see we're Peacers?"

Obviously not, Tor answered silently. Or, more likely, they don't care. His and Rowland's bright yellow Peace Legion overalls were dusty and grimy enough to make them indistinguishable from those worn by the actual combatants in this stupid little war. Besides, everyone was a target here in Town Three.

Flame boiled upwards from the broken-tooth summit of a Tal mind home. A vehicle burned...

Tor shook his head as much to clear the unwelcome memory as recover his balance. He and Rowland pressed on towards the Peace Legion's makeshift field hospital. His face burned. He blinked against the grit. The stretcher was suddenly unbearably heavy, despite the fact that their burden was a child. A badly burned, unconscious, seven year-old girl.

Town Three stank of smoke, death and decay. Tor had become accustomed to the perfumes of the place but never accepting of them. Many of the bodies they passed were of women, children or the elderly. There were militia amongst the dead, yes, but too many of the corpses belonged to the innocent.

Tor was hot and thirsty, baked by New America's

3

merciless larger sun. Its smaller companion was a few degrees above the crest of the purple-hued hills that dominated the view from the end of the shell-cratered main street. Everything would stop when that little blue-white bastard reached its zenith. Even the fighting. The lesser sun might be small, but it was hell-hot. In two hours, everyone would be inside or underground for the four hours it took Star B to cross the sky. Anyone caught out in the open, including un-recovered casualties, would die.

... charred and abandoned marine armour. He saw corpses, all of them human...

More shells thudded into the ruins of the town to Tor's left. The ground shuddered with each impact. He didn't flinch. This was another horror he had become used to.

Not far now. He and Rowland lurched right and into a narrower road. It took them between the scorched and broken faces of standard cuboid colony-start-up domiciles. On most worlds they were replaced within a few years by sturdier, more individualistic buildings. Here, on New America, however, such progress was continually hampered by disputes which too often resulted in armed conflict. Tor had long given up trying to understand who believed what and why it required war to settle an argument or make a point.

The reason for this latest flare-up, as far as he had been able to work it out, was access and control of water and fertile land; in short supply on New America. Corporate imperatives loomed behind the endless conflicts that ravaged the place; denied, of course, but who else had the finances to supply weapons and salary the mercenaries that plagued the planet?

As a Peace Legionnaire, the whys and wherefores of the conflict were none of Tor's concern. The Legion was neutral and independent. They were funded by anonymous donation and brought aid and succour wherever they were needed to whomever needed it. War, natural disaster, accidents in space or planetside, the chances were that there would be Peacers wading waist-high in the carnage. There was probably another Legion Unit treating casualties on the other side of this war.

Or it might be Iaens, of course, bringing healing for the wounded and resurrection for the dead. It depended who the enemy were. There were certainly no Iaens available to aid this side of the conflict.

The Legion was spread thin, with outposts within sub-light, or near-lightspeed reach of most human colonies, but as humankind expanded through the galaxy, that coverage was being stretched towards breaking point.

Minimum service was five years. No questions were asked, either by commanders or comrades. The life was tough and relentless. The casualty rate was high. If you were on the run, the Legion was sanctuary. If it was atonement you sought, the Legion was your priest.

Except, for Tor, redemption was always just out of reach. And now it faded altogether because this war had torn open the barely-healed wounds inflicted on his soul by his sin – an ancient concept, but what was genocide, if not a sin?

As he stumbled the last few metres down the bruised, debris-strewn street to the field hospital, Tor choked on the stink, the devastation, the blood and ruined flesh and, suddenly, could no longer remember where he was. He staggered again, almost collapsed. Psychological weight, suddenly physical.

"Are you hit?" Rowland's alarmed cry. "Kurt, Kurt are you okay?"

Kurt? Who the hell was Kurt? The name was wrong but familiar… Him, it was him. That was who he was here, in the Legion, Kurt Holm. That was it, it all came back to him. He was in the hot, brutal war on New America. Yes, yes… but…

Katherina Molale was here, beside him. How long had she been there? She turned and spoke. Her lips moved but Tor's war-blasted hearing, and the relentless, muffled din of the shelling blocked her words. She smiled and reached for his hand and he released the left handle to take it. The stretcher lurched and swung behind him.

Rowland's shout splintered the illusion. Katherina was smoke, light, shadow. Never there. Tor was wrenched sideways by the weight of the stretcher he now held with one hand. It hit the ground. Rowland swore and yelled and grabbed at the patient to prevent her from rolling free.

Tor stepped away. He tried to clear his head. Others emerged from the dust and ever-present smoke to help. Someone had an arm about his shoulders and was guiding him towards the hospital entrance.

"It's okay. I'm okay." He shrugged the arm away. "I'm not wounded. I'm… "

"You're done," Rowland, at his side and kinder now. She was a good friend. There were times when they had taken their comradeship further than it ought to go. They were human after all, and life as a Peacer was harsh and lonely. "You look terrible, Kurt. Come on. You need to rest."

He didn't fight it, but allowed her to lead him into the hospital. No relief was to be found there, however. The entrance was a portal to Hell. The stink of sweat and human waste, the raw meat odour of torn flesh, spiced with the sharp tangs of medicinal chemicals, the cries and screams, pummelled his senses from all sides. Casualties of war, both guilty and innocent, lay on beds and tables, were propped up in chairs and stretched out on the floor. Harassed Peacer doctors and orderlies picked their way through the carnage. There was a temporary operating theatre in an adjoining area which had once been a classroom. Tor recalled that this was a school, which made the horror of the place somehow more poignant.

Rowland took him through to what might have been a staff room. There was drink and rations laid out on the dusty table at its centre. The windows were all broken and dust danced wildly in the bright beams of sunlight. Rowlands poured coffee, two mugs, one of which she handed to Tor.

"It gets to us all." She sounded weary. Her face was caked with dust. Her hair was escaping its severe ponytail and was dishevelled and matted with yet more dust mixed with tiny fragments of debris. There was blood on her hands and smeared across her filthy Peacer overall. "You're exhausted, Kurt. You need rest. You drive yourself like a madman."

Tor nodded. But this wasn't fatigue. This was flashback and guilt.

The door opened to admit another legionnaire, as dusty, battered and weary as the rest.

"Ah, good, Holm, I've found you." Tor recognised him as Captain Li, the Unit Commander. "Rowland, I need to speak with Holm for a moment."

"Of course, sir." Rowland paused as she made to leave. "Take care of yourself Kurt. Get some rest."

Tor nodded his thanks.

Li took a seat beside him. "You look like hell."

"And you don't, sir?"

"I've just received word that your five years is up. You're done here." Li had been with Tor since the beginning of his exile and failed atonement. He knew exactly who and what he was. "You're free to leave on the next supply lander."

"I'm staying. I just need some sleep. I'll be fine –"

"Tor, listen to me. We have known each other for a long time now. We have been through a lot together, and it has been an honour. You're tireless, courageous to the point of suicidal and have nothing more to prove to me or any of your comrades. But, whatever you are running from, *really* running from, is gaining on you. I've seen it before, many times. It will cause you to slip and fall one day, and Peacers like us only make that sort of mistake once."

And would that be such a bad thing? "I don't want to leave."

"Then you are relieved of your duties on psychological and medical grounds."

"I have nowhere to go. This is my life." Demons were waiting for him out there, in a Hell of guilt and despair.

Li nodded. He leaned forward and frowned, as if

gathering his thoughts before speaking again. "There is a planet, a place, where you might find the peace you're looking for."

"I'm not interested in some retreat."

I don't want contemplation. I don't want silence, because when the noise and fury stop, the horrors crawl in.

"Oh, Mi is no retreat, Tor. Mi is both Heaven and Hell. I have spent time there. I was exhausted, close to breaking down. On Mi, I was healed."

"Nothing can... nothing can wipe this away."

Li clapped a hand on Tor's shoulder. "You don't have a choice. Call it shore leave if you like. I'll order the next supply ship to take you. Mi will consume your pain. I promise."

Storm passed, Tor Danielson picked up his roughly weaved vine net, left his sanctuary and headed for the beach where there would be food. The last of the clouds shredded and dissolved and the sky was clear blue once more. The hurricane force winds had shrunk to a warm breeze that troubled the wild garden of brightly-coloured vegetation through which he walked. The wind tousled his long hair; there were no barbers on Mi. The air carried the clean scent of renewal.

Tor weaved his way through the garden's maze of translucent stems. Its canopy, some three or four metres above his head, consisted of giant blooms and thick, heavy leaves that dripped captured rainwater. Insects swarmed about his legs, disturbed from their nectar gathering at the smaller plants of the garden's undergrowth. Larger invertebrates droned around the higher blooms. The creatures' metallic carapaces glittered when struck by the restored sunlight. Their wings were a blur of magnificent colours.

Tor shared their imperatives; eat, seek a mate, copulate, and breed before oblivion. Their impulses and primitive thoughts swirled into his mind and through his entire body. They danced on his nerves, tightened his reflexes. Their half-formed joys, and their threats, were his. He had learned how to absorb just enough to remain connected to what he believed to be the planet's id, and how to push aside the irrelevant. It had been overwhelming at first, but now it was a comfort. Tor was alone here on Mi, but never lonely.

He emerged from the garden onto the lip of the thirty-metre cliff that dropped to a narrow beach. Then there was the sea, a vast, limitless expanse that stretched towards the unthinkably distant horizon. Currents of light wound procession-like through its surface. It was water, yes, but laced with other, stranger components. The sea, here on Mi, was a thing of secrets. As deadly as it was beautiful. Gigantic worms burrowed through its night-black depths, huge cephalopods occasionally breached to offer tantalisingly brief views of their vast flanks and lashing tentacles. White crested waves rolled slowly shore-wards to break lazily on the far-below beach where leathery, pterodactylane flyers circled and dipped to pick morsels from the ocean's heaving skin.

A rockfall provided a way down. It was a hard, perilous descent but one he was used to. He was naked, skin hardened from exposure to the weather and physical battering he had taken during those first few months of his sojourn here, but he was still vulnerable to injury from the sharp rocks and loose shale. His body was mapped with scars, bruises, and half-healed cuts and grazes. No broken bones, thank God. A fracture would be the death of him.

Every paradise had its serpent. Mi had more than Tor could ever count.

Once on the beach, Tor kept a respectful distance from the spray-flecked charge and retreat of the sea. The sun bathed his face. The stony sand was warm under his feet. The flying beasts swept him with brief shadows.

A new wave of connections rose from the waters. Hungers, terrors. And that other, a huge presence, perhaps the ocean itself, or something immense that made its home deep in its heart.

He set to work gathering up the strands of bright emerald seaweed the storm had washed up, hidden under the vegetation were protein-rich shellfish and other invertebrates. It didn't take long to fill the net and once he had gathered sufficient food, Tor hunted for anything that might be useful, branches for firewood and tools, other plants that could be used for weaving or effecting repairs to his home. He paused every now and then to breathe the salty air, revel in the sunlight and listen to the planet. The voices, the rough-hewn emotions, the scents and colours and electric thrum of Mi and all it contained and supported, burned through him. It blotted out thought and identity. He felt his own borders and peripheries blur and dissolve. He closed his eyes and *saw*.

Something.

A vibration, an intrusion, a flicker, a glint, small but enough to make him look up.

A tiny, bright spark streaked across the empty sky, leaving a hair-thin trail of fire in its wake. It grew brighter and larger as it arced landwards then disappeared from view over the lip of the cliff. A moment later there was sound, a deep meld of roar and hum. Familiar enough to scrape away at the protective layers Mi's energies had formed about his mind and reveal unwelcome memories and associations; lander, spacecraft, others, intruders, the shadow.

Weighted down by foreboding, Tor jogged back to the rockfall and began the climb. The comforting maelstrom of connections with Mi and its myriad lives dissolved and left him weary and apprehensive. He wanted to hide but knew he had to face this intrusion and whatever it brought in its wake. The net was suddenly heavy and cumbersome. The rocks were hard and brutal under his hands and feet.

Other sensations flared bright among the connections between himself and Mi. A threat. A close threat, real and immediate.

He turned and saw them in that odd out-of-the-corner-of-the-eye way danger is first detected. A movement, quick. Tor looked across to his left and there they were. Stick men, scuttling across the cliff face. Three, four of them. Gleaming, almost metallic black, quick, humanoid-yet-spiderish.

It was terrifying but also exhilarating. The adrenalin hit, the need to survive. The stickmen would tear him apart if they caught him. They would strip the flesh from his body and suck the marrow from his bones. They were hunger and instinct. They were relentless and merciless.

Tor hauled himself upwards. He dragged with his arms and pushed with his legs. He could see the stick men in his mind's eye. Up. Up, you bastard. Come on. Come on.

His calloused hands grabbed at the rock. His feet, bleeding now, scrabbled and dug blindly for footholds.

Up, up, up.

Oh, this was good. This was real. Life, death, part of the whole. If he died, then so be it. That was the way of things here. Tor had always known that Mi would kill him one day, perhaps it was today. He relished the chase, the pound of his heart, the laboured drag of air into his lungs, the fight, the flight, the fear, the euphoria of existence on this knife blade between life and oblivion. *This*, he understood.

The first of the stickmen was about twenty metres away, a little below, slowed by lack of foot and handholds in that particular stretch of cliff face. Once it reached the rockfall, however, it would be on him in seconds. Another was gaining on the first, a larger, obviously stronger specimen.

Pack animals they might be, the stickmen didn't work together once the hunt began. They were fractious and self-centred and not averse to tearing each other to death if one of them got in the way of a meal. Tor had seen their murderous crimes of passion numerous times, on his many treks to the beach or inland. That knowledge was his only weapon.

He stopped. Every instinct screamed at him to climb, to escape. Instead he offered himself. A baited trap.

The nearer stickman became frantic and risked all by speeding up its awkward crawl across the cliff face, but its larger rival was faster. It surged towards Tor. It loomed behind its oblivious, hunger-maddened rival and struck. Claw-slashes tore flesh and spattered dark blood across the rocks. The smaller squealed and hit back at its attacker.

Tor drove himself upwards in a desperate scramble towards the cliff edge.

A few more grabs, pulls and kicks and pushes. Up, up, bloody up.

He thrust his head over the lip. His arms windmilled to grab at handfuls of grass and tough surface roots then half-dragged and half-boosted himself up and onto his belly. No time for a rest. Tor scrambled to his feet and ran into the garden. He weaved between the flowers, listening, sensing, reaching out for any indication that the stickmen were on his heels.

He reached the cave.

Which was less cavern and more a hole in the ground at the base of a flower-covered hillock deep in the garden. The entrance was concealed behind a tightly knit curtain of flowered vines. Tor drew them apart and crawled in then curled protectively about his basket of supplies and waited as the vines re-wove themselves back into a near impenetrable barrier.

He should eat but he had no appetite. Instead he struggled to heal a sudden rupture in his psyche and staunch the seep of unwanted memories. It was the lander, a splinter that dug deep into his sub-conscious.

He was a murderer. He had taken thousands of lives, alien and incomprehensible perhaps, but life was life. And mixed amongst them, dying with them in that moment of white-hot nuclear hell, were two humans, one of them his lover.

Katherina Molale.

Former… no, he still loved her. He always would.

It had not been face-to-face, that act of mass extinction. That genocide. It had been detached, glimpsed from above as a series of bright, silent flashes far away on Ia's surface. Little specks of light observed by Secretary for Interplanetary Affairs Tor Danielson as he was slammed into his seat on-board a marine flyer and hurled skywards from the planet's surface. Tor had stared out of the side port and watched the white streaks of missile exhausts. They were almost beautiful as they arced Ia-wards. A few seconds of nothing as they disappeared into the glow of the planet's reflected sunlight. Then those pretty, flower-like flares, so small and insignificant.

A clean strike. The warheads configured to restrict the apocalypse to a tightly defined space, the war-ruined Tal city. The home of the original inhabitants of Ia. It had

taken only a few minutes for the truth of those
unimportant little flickers to filter into Tor's
consciousness and slather his soul in blood-red guilt.

By the time the starship *Kissinger* reached Earth, Tor
was a drug-fuelled automaton. He functioned, he smiled
and heard speech issue from his mouth, while, trapped
within its narcotic cage, the frightened, broken ape raged
and threw itself against the iron bars until its bones were
broken and it bled from a thousand wounds.

Tor realised that he was on his knees, exhausted from
crying. His nose dripped snot, his eyes stung from tears.
He was unable to move. His skin tingled and burned. He
wanted to run to hide. He wanted to stay where he was
and let his body and mind crumble to dust and to be gone.

And that was when the voices crept into his awareness.
No words, but sounds, feelings, sighs perhaps, music, but
no music he would comprehend. The planet spoke to him.
The planet eased his burden, dug deep and healed.

Tor stirred and forced himself to eat, then left the cave,
to seek out who ever had invaded his refuge. He headed
inland, following the path laid down by the planet's id.
There was something artificial and intrusive on its flesh.
The instinct-driven were afraid and watched from afar.
Mi's plant-life screamed warnings along its web of
intertwined roots, hormone pulses and electrochemical
bursts that shivered through Tor's nerves as a series of
tiny shocks.

He left the garden and trekked over a rockier terrain,
where the vegetation was scrubbier. The landscape was
broken by a haphazard scatter of building-sized rocks,
stratified, flat-topped and thrust out of the ground by some
ancient seismic cataclysm. Mountains, blued by distance,
walled-in the horizon. Their flanks were darkened by
dense forest. Those forests unnerved Tor and he kept away
from them. The washed-out dome of the larger of the three
daytime moons lowered over the far-off peaks.

There, down where the rough landscape swept into a
shallow plain, a lander waited. It was a two-man space
boat, squat, ugly and still hot enough from its re-entry to

blur the surrounding air into a hazy dance. Its ramp was down and a figure waited. As Tor drew closer he became increasingly certain that he recognised the visitor. A man in a utilitarian overall. Tool belt, some weapon in his hands; a burner. Then vague recognition turned to shock. Tor was suddenly disorientated. He stopped walking. He tried to comprehend the fact that the visitor was himself.

Tor Danielson.

*

I am, and am not, Tor Danielson. Once I, well Tor, was World President and Governor of All Humankind's Colonies. He/I had the highest position any human being can attain and yet, here I am, standing on a rocky plain on a planet most people don't even believe exists. Mi, a legend, a hope, Heaven, Hell, both.

No, Tor, don't run, wait, listen. I'll drop the burner. There. Did you see me do it? Did you hear it thud when it hit the ground? See, now I'm empty handed. You can come at me with the rock you have in your fist and there's nothing I can do about it.

I understand. You are frightened… no, that's not it. You're angry that I, *we*, are here. Me, your replacement, we, the people and forces I represent. That you *believe* I represent. Am I right, Tor? Well, I'm not here for the reason you think I am, but you're not convinced, are you.

You are also Tor Danielson. I am you and yet, not you. You are me and yet, not me. I am clean shaven. I'm wearing clothes. My hair is neat. You are naked, your hair long, your face obscured by a shaggy beard. You are dirty, battered, lean and tough. There is something in your eye, in your posture, a wildness, an energy, alertness, I don't know exactly, and yet you are at peace. I'm nervous. Fearful of what I might find on this planet, and of what I have been created to do.

You are Tor Danielson. I am the copy. A fake. A stand-in. This is your world. If we fought, the same two bodies and minds, you would win. But, replica or not, to recreate a human being, to truly rebuild, you have to mix in all the ingredients.

Including memories. But memories are of no use without the authenticity of feelings. Of the emotion they evoke and revive. I have those feelings, to a certain extent, but it is all artifice. What is real for me and what is programmed?

The CellTech Corporation were clever. They included repression in my make-up. The memories I needed to function were available, but those I didn't need, in theirs and the World Council's opinion, at least, were buried and irretrievable. Which is why I am here.

I am not the first Tor Danielson proto born in a CellTech seeder tank. I was formed from the biological template their technicians created for those other Tors. Those protos that replaced you as President and puppet. My creators, parents, call them what you will, didn't have the skill to change the template, so that repression is still in place, even though they are vital to my purpose.

My birth?

Traumatic. I remember flashes of consciousness during those final days in my seeder tank. They terrified me. I did not understand what was happening. Images, feelings, sounds that had no context for me, no meaning. Shapes, colours, events. I tried to retreat from them. I tried to escape but they came from inside me. How can you run from something that is you?

Gradually, I was able to make a little sense of what I experienced. It is a necessary part of the seeder tank process. The proto-being grown there has to have some understanding of the world they are about to enter. Many of the shapes were human faces. The sounds, their voices. Two of them were constant companions during those last days and hours before my birth. Both women, one older than the other, but connected, to each other and to me.

Annika, that was the older of the two. Eva, the younger. I could not comprehend, how she came from me and from Annika, but I felt intense emotion every time her face and voice filtered into my dreams.

I don't know if they were actually dreams, but there is no other way to describe the visions I experienced in the tank.

Annika, yes, she evoked a similar emotion, but it was tempered by... I wasn't sure. Fear? Anger?

Those were the most intense moments of my prenatal madness. As neural connections were made and impulses sparked their way through my newly formed brain. There were other memories, of course. War, conflict and upheaval across my home world, Earth. The ragged procession of refugees that poured into the cold, mountainous place I understood was my home when I was young. I experienced compassion. And exhaustion. I worked for the government, something junior and unimportant, but it enabled me to help those people, doing all I could until I almost collapsed. I was noticed, however, promoted, swept up through the ranks, ever higher until I stood on the summit where the ground is treacherous and the air thin.

Except it wasn't *me* who did that. I had a sense that these were not my own memories. I know now that they are yours Tor. You helped those people. You sacrificed your health to bring them succour. You oversaw the building of camps. You organised medical care, food supplies. All of it. That's where you met Annika wasn't it. She was an aid worker, her face smudged, her hair awry, tired and pale and yet the most beautiful young woman you had ever seen. A shared compassion, wasn't it, shared compassion that became a shared passion.

You are a great man, Tor Danielson. You, not me. I am your shadow.

There is something else though, isn't there. I understand it now, but for a long time, it was an irritant, a closed room, a place that would terrify me if I ever attempted to approach. Even then. In the tank, naked, afloat in amniotic fluids, pierced by pipes and cables, my body wracked with involuntary twitching and convulsions. Even then I was in fear of that place in your/my psyche that I could never visit, because to do so would tear me apart.

Then I was born.

Christ, Tor, thank every deity you can name that you don't remember your own birth. For one moment there is comfort, security, the small, reassuring world of the tank, the next, a violent tug and backwards wrench. You fall, unable to stop as the fluid rushes around you like a torrent. Voices pummelled my ears. Rough hands grabbed and held me. Then the pipes and tubes were ripped from my flesh. That kind of pain and terror are best smothered and repressed. Mine are the stuff of my nightmares.

Exposed, alone, I was surrounded by strangers with cold eyes above masks that made them monstrous and inhuman. I was strapped down. Needles, and other procedures were inflicted on me. Rough and hurried. Then it was out into the world. Crying, screaming and struggling.

Alone.

I am, and am not, Tor Danielson.

And I have come to unlock that room full of darkness.

"Tor."

*

"Tor," the other Tor said, the one by the lander ramp. The Other. "It's okay, I'm not here to hurt you."

His voice. Christ, his own voice.

The Other sounded as shaken as he was.

"Go away," Tor said.

"Please, listen –"

"No, leave me alone. Just go."

"I'm not going to do that, not until we've spoken."

"About what? What is there to talk about?" His voice felt rough and unused. He experienced an odd inferiority to the much smarter, sleeker version of himself. "Who the fuck are you, anyway?" Stupid question. He knew the answer already.

A moment, then, "Former President, Tor Danielson."

"*Former* President?"

"But still Governor of All Human Colonies. It's a long story, Tor," the Other said. "But the story is coming to its end. The Alliance are demanding justice for what happened on Ia –"

Tor shook his head. He backed away. "No, no. I don't want the past."

"It's never the past, Tor."

He ran then, back up the shallow slope. The Other shouted to him to stop, to listen, but Tor wanted none of it. He drove himself hard. He couldn't think, but knew that he had to get away from the nightmare that had invaded his refuge. He slipped and stumbled as he scrambled up the slope then glanced back. The other was following, at an easy jog, calling out for him to wait.

Tor would outrun him. The other would become lost in the Garden. The planet was dangerous. He would be hunted, attacked, killed even. The thought of that gave Tor pause. He couldn't let the man die.

Yes, he could. The Other was on Mi by his own choice. He wanted to take him away from here. Tor couldn't bear the thought of that. He reached the top of the slope then bounded across the rocky, uneven space towards the Garden. He pushed himself on, surprised at how fit and nimble he had become. Exhilarated by the chase, he almost laughed, then remembered that his hunter wasn't looking to run him down and eat him. His hunter wanted to drag him back to Hell.

The edge of the Garden was close.

The light shifted towards evening gold. It would be night soon. Mi was dangerous by day, but it was lethal at night.

He reached the Garden and didn't hesitate, but pushed on into the tangled maze of giant stems. The shadows were made dense by the failing light. The Other would never find him in here. The place was alive with predators and their prey. His head was filled with their struggles, to find food, to escape. He felt their urgency and it fired his own. He could feel where the hunters were hiding or stalking and swerved to avoid them. Evening insects swarmed into huge living whirlwinds, tiny sparks of consciousness that bit and stung but caused Tor no other harm.

Not far now. He stumbled into a space where the taller flowers were sparser, and almost ran into the flanks of a huge, soft-fleshed worm-like plant eater. The thing was burrowing into the soft ground, its work done for the day and its belly full. Its forward sections were already deep beneath the loamy soil, but enough of its body remained exposed for it to be vulnerable to predators for whom it would provide days of nourishment.

Tor wished it good luck as he dodged around it and pressed on. There was some answering thrum in his mind, perhaps a return greeting, or a shudder of fear. It was hard to tell.

The air chilled. The shadows lengthened further.

The leaves and the undergrowth rustled. There was no breeze, which meant that it had to be some animal. Runners probably. Yes, runners. He tasted their hunger. They were pack hunters, many-legged and fast. Tor took another wide diversion. He could never survive a chase or fight with them. Discretion was most definitely the best part of valour when they were on the prowl.

"Tor. Stop. Tor, please."

Christ, how the hell had the Other managed to find him so quickly?

Here, in the Garden, in the near-dark.

Tor experienced a moment of despair. There was little point in fleeing any further. The Other obviously possessed some form of tracking device. There was only one way to escape this. The realisation hit him, a brutal blow to the heart. He stumbled to a halt and spun about until he faced the direction in which the runners could be found. He should seek them out and let them put an end to this. He would die on Mi. He would not leave. He would not end his life anywhere else. The thought of it was unbearable.

He felt them. He knew them. He was them.

Close now. Tor made no attempt at stealth, instead, he

careered through the Garden towards the runners. He
crashed and blundered. He wanted them and the peace
they would bring. One moment of pain and violence then
it would be done.

Their hunger, the near madness of the hunt, exploded
into his head. It was terrifying enough to bring him to a
halt. What was he doing? This wouldn't save him. This
was the coward's way. This was idiocy. He could shake-
off and lose the Other easily enough. He froze and
shallowed his breathing. The creatures faltered. They
hunted through vibration. His stillness made him
invisible. He willed his pulse to slow. The runners
possessed sensitivities to the heavy thud of a heart.

More crashing and shouting. the Other, making himself
a target. He would have to fend for himself. Tor drew
back slowly, carefully and listened. The silent tension
between predators and their now motionless prey was
over in a moment. The undergrowth hissed and crackled
as they erupted into a scuttering sprint away from Tor and
towards the clumsy blundering of his doppelganger.

When he was sure it was safe to do so, Tor moved on,
making for his cave, certain that he would receive no
more attention from his visitor, for the night at least. He
experienced a pang of guilt for leaving him at the mercy
of the runners, but the survival imperative quickly
crushed any regrets.

*

Oh Christ.

There must be ten of them, probably more. They erupt
into the disc of light cast by my head torch and they are
demons from Hell. Centipedes, that's the nearest I can get
to a description. Countless legs, sinuous, segmented
bodies and heads that look like, and are a similar size to,
crocodiles, all jaws, needle teeth and bulbous compound
eyes.

I heard them, crashing around, but was too sure of my
weapon to concern myself. My attention was on the DNA

scanner, on keeping up with Real Tor as he weaved and jinked through this bizarre garden of giant flowers and weeds. I was aware of animal life, but closed to the possibility of predation.

This moment, is filled with terror and despair and, oddly, fascination. The things move fast. They explode towards me. They become everything.

Worse, I feel their frantic hunger, the insanity of it. Nothing will stop them. They *will* eat. They *will* tear and devour. My mouth is suddenly flooded with liquid. I am salivating. I am actually salivating over my own raw flesh.

The burner. I have a burner. Get it, come on, *come on*.

Scrabble it out of its belt holster. Is it ready to fire? I can't remember if the safety is on or off.

No time to check. Don't think. Don't plan or question.

I fall back. Those jaws stretch wide, too wide, and thrust at me and I smell the stink of the thing. I see a tongue, or tentacle or something worse uncoil from among that forest of teeth.

The burner, for God's sake –

I have it. In my right fist. Heavy, warm. Ready. Please God let it be ready.

A flash of light. A streak of laser-guided heat. A screech as the head of the closest of the monsters boils and bursts. Its body thrashes and driven by its momentum slams into me and knocks me aside and onto my back. I fall into the soft embrace of a mass of small flowers. Tiny flying creatures erupt from the broken plants. They are vividly coloured, like minute prisms, and snatch my attention from the reality of my situation.

The headless body of the burned monster writhes and bucks. The others hurtle over it and become tangled and panicked. They snap at one another. Fights ensue. The rest of the pack divide about the horror. I press myself into the leaves and against the soft ground beneath. There are thorns that tear at my overall and break my skin. I don't care. I can't breathe.

I must not move.

Not that I could even if I wanted to. I am paralysed and shattered with fear as one of the things scuttles over me. I am caged by its insectile legs, buried beneath its train-like body. It's done in a moment and yet, it is forever.

I must not move. They cannot sense you if you remain absolutely still.

The creatures who are still wrestling over and around the corpse of their comrade seem oblivious to my presence now. I suspect cannibalism.

Now I can crawl away, slowly and carefully.

How did I know to remain motionless? Something in my head, a voice yet not a voice. Unnerving, but not to be pondered right now.

I check myself over. Apart from the cuts and abrasions, there seem to be no other ill-effects. I struggle to my feet and grab at a giant flower stem for support. I need to get back to the lander and treat these wounds. Even if there is no toxin there will be infection.

I draw the DNA scanner from my utility belt and set it to read my own traces and guide me back through the flower forest towards my ship. I will try again in the morning. It has a range of 100km. No matter how far the Real Tor travels tonight, I doubt it will be far enough for me to not track him down in the morning.

The garden is alive with sound. Things rustle through the undergrowth and flap overhead. I hear shrieks of fear and pain, I hear a snarl too close for comfort. I am alert however, the burner ready.

There is something else, that sense, that presence in my mind. It is as if the planet is aware of me, and that I am picking up the thoughts and instincts of the fauna, and some of the flora, on this world. It is diffuse, but I suspect that it will grow stronger the longer I am here. It feels and sounds more like a collection of voices. Perhaps this is how Real Tor has survived here for so long. He has become attuned to the life around him. Perhaps he can hear, see and feel the presence of danger, which gives him a chance to get out of its way.

Something squeals. The sound porcine and unpleasant.

There is an answering shriek. I hear snuffling. Something can smell me. All I want now is to be out from amongst these bloody flowers. I increase my pace, aware that I am making a lot of noise.

A gap, ahead, a lighter shade of night. I want to run for it but something holds me back. I move carefully. I realise that I still have the burner in my hand. A last resort. I don't want to shed any more blood tonight.

The garden's border is tantalisingly close. Every instinct within me is urging me to make a dash for it, but what happens once I'm out there? There are rocks and shadows, yes, but I will be just as exposed to predators out there as I am in here. I doubt I will be able to outrun anything that wants to eat me, so I need to use whatever stealth my clumsy arms and legs can manage.

More snuffling. A shriek. Much nearer than the last time. Something is closing in.

God, I want to be on the lander again. I want to be safe. For whatever is out there, I'm food, no more. Dead, alive, it doesn't matter. Again, I experience a glimpse of its hunger. A fleeting sense.

It's coming; running, slithering, desperate, a living weapon of muscle and flesh and need.

I can't tell from which direction. It's all around me. My violent, horrible death, a few metres away. Movement. I can see it. No, shadow.

I can't bear this.

I fire into the darkness. I rake the stems and leaves, and the black places between them with burner flame. I wrench myself through a full circle and drag the dazzling shaft of hot light with me. Things squeal and howl. Stems are sliced and giant blooms crash to the ground. I smell burning flesh.

Then run.

I burst from the garden's edge and pound over the hard, uneven ground between the flat-topped rocks that separate the garden from the plain where the lander waits. A huge moon hangs above the horizon and sheds stark, silver-white light over the landscape. I glimpse shapes that bound beside me on either side. They are thin, like stickmen drawn by children. Their legs are over-long, their emaciated torsos thrust forward, almost horizontal, like birds, and balanced by long, rat-like tails. Their arms are tucked under their chests. Whatever they are, I'm sure they are dangerous. They are flickers in the corner of my vision. They are the spur that keeps me running long after my lungs burn and I am clawing for breath.

Voices roar in my head. No words, no sense, but there is anger, at me, at the wanton destruction I wrought back there in the garden. I am a splinter in Mi's skin, a parasite, unwanted, despised. I am ugly and crass. I am as violent as the denizens of this world, but my violence is dirty. It is an affront. It brings imbalance where there is balance.

"I'm sorry… I'm sorry… " I don't know when I began my sobbed apology to the rock and vegetation and fauna of Mi. It is irrational and ridiculous, but somehow, it salves my conscience as I run for my life.

I weave and foolishly seek shadows to throw off my pursuers. Foolish because those patches of inky blackness may hide other horrors. Everything on this world is closing in on me.

One of those stick-like bipeds, directly ahead, coming for me from the dark cleft between two of those flat-topped rocks. I can't see it but I know it's there, head down, barrelling in for the kill.

I know. I *feel* it.

I veer left, trip and stumble then fire, splashing heat over the ground a little ahead of the creature. I hear its squeal of fear and, for an instant, experience the terror of the weapon's flash and resulting heat wave. The warning shot is enough.

On I go. Thorned scrub rips at my legs. More cuts and scratches. I run as best I can, a shambolic stagger, tripping on the rocks, my limbs heavy, my head swimming.

And, suddenly, I'm on the lip of the valley, and there, the lander, now lit up to guide me home.

I sense the stick men behind me, coming fast. I throw

myself down on the hill, slipping and skidding in a shower of scree. Pebbles and small rocks roll beside me. My crazed, barely-controlled sprint down the slope gives me the momentum I need to drive me across the flat. The things are close behind. Any moment now, any moment I will feel a claw –

Up the ramp, up, adrenalin overcomes exhaustion and pain. Hatch open then closing as I fall inside. It slams shut and something collides with it. I hear scratching and squealing. It goes on for ever.

Again, on my knees, hauling air into my tortured lungs, I ask myself how the hell does Real Tor survive here?

Silence returns. Hopefully, that means that those stick monsters have gone. I don't know how I'm still alive. I wasn't birthed to be a soldier or explorer, I keep fit, but not dangerous environment-fit. I am formed from the template of a middle-aged politician, a President, in fact, not an adventurer, although the ghost of that rugged, younger Tor Danielson who gave his all for the displaced and broken, still haunts these cells and muscles. And didn't Real Tor spend five years in the Peace Legion? That's no life for a soft-skinned, delicately-petalled bureaucrat. I share those hardier genes. It's just a matter of finding them and sparking them into life.

A fire that might be ignited sooner rather than later if I spent too much time here on Mi.

I'll try to find and communicate with Real Tor again tomorrow. I need to rest, although a part of me dreads sleep. That's when the memories surface, Real Tor's memories, vivid and terrible. I have no reason to feel guilty and yet I do. Perhaps it is because I am Tor Danielson and am sure that if I was placed in the same position as Real Tor, I would have made the same decisions as he did. Exhaustion overwhelms me, however, so I huddle into one of the vehicle's seats and give in to it.

Sleep brings dreams; emotions, images, sounds. A woman who is not Annika. A woman I/he loves. A woman I/he killed.

And the madness of my sudden birth.

And the torrent of memories and knowledge that flooded into me at that moment. The people who arrived in that empty, clinical white room a few hours later found me huddled in a corner trembling and sobbing because I did not understand this person I am. They wore white laboratory overalls. They seemed kind and tried to entice me from my hiding place with gentle words of encouragement. One of them, a young woman, knelt in front of me, smiled, and held out her hand. I shrank away. I couldn't think. I couldn't stop the noise and images and feelings that spiralled through my mind. None of them made sense. They were fragments that tumbled into focus then instantly dissolved to be replaced by another and another.

At last a woman wearing a business tunic broke in and shooed the others out. Once we were alone, she crouched down, just as the other woman had. I let her take my hand because I knew her, because her name emerged from my newly-minted memory.

"Lisa Kavanagh."

Her smile broadened. "Yes, yes, that's who I am. I work for you, Tor. I was your Press Secretary." Ah, yes, she was the one who protected me from the people who wanted to bring me down with words and images. "Although, that isn't a job anymore. The press on Earth are no longer interested in Tor Danielson. These days, they're told what to be interested in."

Her words made little sense, but there was something I did understand. "We are friends," I said.

She seemed moved by that and nodded, as if unable to speak.

"You were hurt." The memory was stark and violent. An explosion, fire, falling...

"I was, but I'm all right now." She frowned. "What do you remember about that?"

"Nothing... it's confusing."

"Do you know what you are?"

"Human."

"True, but what is your role as a human?"

The answer was almost within my grasp. It coalesced with painful slowness into something that made sense. I was above them, a leader and yet felt as if I was a child. Someone who knew a great deal and yet very little.

"I am the President of… of Humankind, of Earth and Governor of all its Colonies."

"Not anymore. I'm sorry. You were a powerful man, Tor." Now she looked unhappy.

"I don't feel powerful."

"Tor… you never did, which is why you were such a good politician… " Her voice trailed away. "What else do you know? What else seems important to you?"

"A woman. Annika. She's… she's my wife. My companion and friend, no, more than that. I feel strongly about her."

"You love her."

Did I? I was unsure because it felt as if there was someone else that I loved. I couldn't name her or even see her in my mind, not in the way I saw Annika. There was another young woman that seemed part of her, us. Perhaps that was who I really loved. No, this other was my daughter. Eva, that was her name. I felt strongly towards her but not in the way I felt about Annika and… it was no use. This other woman was a shadow, whoever she was, gone, painted out. All I knew was that the thought of her brought a huge sadness to me. She was part of that dark place I couldn't see into.

Lisa began to talk. She helped me to understand the things I already knew but could not fully grasp.

Then she said; "You are not the first Tor Danielson. There have been three. You are the fourth. And you are the one who is going to save us."

"I don't understand."

The sadness was back. She blinked and I saw that she was fighting tears. "Tor, you are to be a sacrifice."

It was while Lisa and two security guards, my security guards, escorted me to my apartments, that I understood that we were on a space station. It was when we passed various ports and viewing windows that I caught glimpses of the frighteningly vast blackness outside. When I was delivered into my apartment's spacious lounge, my breath was snatched away by the dazzling blue curve of a planet visible through its huge wall window. I knew, instinctively, however, that it was not Earth.

Lisa caught me staring, placed a hand on my shoulder, which I found astonishingly comforting, and said, "That's Sirius 12. It's the capital world of the Federation of Human Colonies. You... I mean, President Danielson is in exile here. The colonies see you as their Governor, so you still have that part of your job title at least. Earth is... troubled, in turmoil."

I felt sorrow for Tor's home world. The love of Earth, a world I had never seen, was rooted deep into my borrowed psyche. Lisa placed a hand on my shoulder. The gesture comforted me.

"The Federation wants independence from an Earth no longer fit to administer its colonies. And they want to rejoin the Alliance of Planets."

Lisa's words awakened memories and understanding. Incomplete, but enough for me to grasp the meaning of what she was telling me. It was a lot to absorb, but I fed on it greedily because knowledge brought stability. I began to comprehend who and what I was and the world into which I had been thrown.

"The Alliance are amenable to the move," Lisa said. "There is just one condition –"

"Tor?"

I turned away from the view to see that a tall, elegant woman had entered the room. She stared but made no move towards me. There was no affection in her voice. Memories of her embrace and her kisses flooded in. There had been intimacy between us once, intense, joyous, but no longer. Now, she seemed afraid of me. Then she started to cry.

"I can't do this anymore," she said. "Lisa, please don't make me."

"I'm sorry Annika, we all are, but there's no other way. It has to look real. The Alliance won't accept it if it isn't. This will be the last time, I promise you. It's almost over."

Annika straightened, her face hard now. I took a step towards her. I needed to feel her in my arms. I needed to be close to her, because I was, and am, Tor Danielson, no matter that I was formed in a seeder tank. I was Tor Danielson and I loved the woman who now backed away from me as if I was a monster.

"Leave me alone. Do you understand?"

"Annika… "

"Do not touch me, or come near me or my daughter –"

Our daughter, Eva was *our* daughter.

"Leave us alone." And she fled back to her own rooms, leaving me confused and bereft.

*

In his cave, as safe as it was possible to be on Mi, Tor forced himself to eat. He lit a small fire by the entrance for cooking and heat. The flames caused the vine curtain to untangle and retreat to the edges of the opening. That was okay because no living thing on Mi would venture anywhere near a fire. He used the flints he had gathered on one of his foraging excursions to light it and fed it with sticks and plant fibres he had stored and dried. These were skills he had learned as a child on Earth, when he had been the member of an organisation that taught and encouraged self-reliance and initiative. He couldn't recall the name of the organisation. These memories might be foggy, distant, as most of them were now, but he knew that he had been happy then.

His memories were not lost. They were suppressed, willingly. He had learned quickly to allow the voices of Mi to seep into every part of his mind and they had acted as a balm once he had understood that the planet's id, collective mind, whatever it might be, meant him no harm.

Most of the noise was made by the consciousnesses of the flora and fauna that existed here. Most of it was instinct and need, fear and a primitive joy. There was unity and yet little mercy. The predators slaughtered and devoured the predated, the predated slaughtered and devoured the plant life, which, in turn, fought wars, in its silent, imperceptible way, over access to sunlight and fertile soil. There was balance, however, and an odd, half-formed, communal understanding that this was the way of things.

Something else lurked behind the cacophony of feelings and imperatives, something larger and sentient. Its presence was not obvious, rather, it was only there when not actively sought. It was like a low frequency rumble, distant thunder, a flicker of lightning, there, gone. There was comfort in that background thrum, but also the unsettling notion that whatever it was, it was aware of Tor, of who and what he was and why he was here. He could not discern whether it tolerated him, was disinterested or angry. So far, there had been nothing to make him feel that it meant him any harm.

Tor had come to believe that the heart of the presence lay in those huge forests that darkened the foothills of the mountain ranges bordering this part of the planet. The closest was off to the north of the Garden. He had trekked to within a few miles of the place in the early days of his sojourn here. He had taken to exploring as far afield as he dared go and learned a lot of near-fatal, but valuable, lessons during those journeys. He made it to within a kilometre of the forest but could not bring himself to go any closer. That wall of huge trees had seemed impenetrable, the intensity of the voices and life-energy that rolled out of its shadows overwhelming and deafening.

So, Tor ate the shellfish and seaweed he had gathered from the shore in what now felt like a lifetime ago, and drank water he had collected from the huge concave leaves of what he called bowl plants. Satiated, he stretched out on the loamy floor to sleep. He would have to move on in the morning. He hoped that if he left before dawn, he would have a head start on the Other. If he drove himself hard, he would hopefully move out of reach of whatever tracking devices the bastard was using.

Provided the Other didn't have the same idea.

He might, also, be dead.

Sleep was elusive.

Memories pushed through Mi's discordant but soothing music.

And guilt that Tor had left his doppelganger at the mercy of the runners and whatever else hunted in the Garden at night.

No, he wouldn't torture himself over this. He had not invited the Other here. There was no reason for the Council or whoever else had sent him, to hunt him down. The Other was proof that if they needed a Tor Danielson, they could simply create one.

But why send him here? Alone? The President of Earth and Governor of its Colonies, dumped, here, on a lethal, little-known planet? No security guards or advisors. Dressed like an interplanetary surveyor. What the hell had happened to humankind?

See? Already those other ugly thoughts and concerns were crowding in on his peace. Soon it wouldn't simply be puzzles and questions, it would be memories and guilt and then the madness would return.

Tor rolled onto his back and listened to Mi. As he opened his mind to the noise, the babble and chaos, a recollection broke through, unwelcome but too vivid to douse.

The voyage home from Ia.

When.

Safe at last on the *Kissinger*, Tor swallowed his first handful of the tranquilisers and anti-depressants prescribed by the World Council-appointed medic, assigned to care for the diplomatic team. The *Kissinger* was thirty-six hours from quantum jump. One-and-half days in which to face the consequences of his decision down on Ia.

Genocide.

Expulsion from the Alliance of Planets.

All resulting from a union with an invading force who had lied both to him and to humankind in general. Unless the Council had known all along of course. Oh, come on, the rest of the Council had already made up their minds to unleash genocide on the Tal. After all, they had authorised a covert operation on the planet, on behalf of the Iaens, long before Tor arrived.

But then, hadn't he, Tor, purchased humankind a magnificent gift with his blood money? Immortality. Healing for the seriously sick and wounded. Resurrection for the newly dead. Surely that outweighed the brutality of his order to unleash Armageddon on an alien species so different, so difficult to comprehend, and who claimed to be the wronged party but might have been lying.

No, they weren't lying. Katherina Molale was scrupulous in her journalism. If she claimed to have discovered the truth about the Iaens and the Tal, then it *was* the truth.

Katherina.

A featherlight kiss in the dark, a softness and kindness and excitement he had never known before –

Dead.

Dead.

By his hand. He had murdered her.

Around and around it went, a maelstrom of horror, self-loathing, self-justification, euphoria that he could snatch his daughter back from the jaws of death, then horror once more. Only the drugs could still the storm. Only the drugs numbed the pain and smoothed the jagged edges of his conscience.

Then, four hours before jump, he received a visit.

"Sir, news from Earth."

Tor recognised the voice but, surely, it couldn't be who he thought it was.

"Lisa?"

"Yes, Sir, please let us in. It's urgent, and I mean *urgent*."

Lisa?

Tor ordered the door to open and she was there. Whole and seemingly healthy. Lisa Kavanagh, his Press Secretary and Attack Dog. Tor was on his feet, confused, delighted, overwhelmed by the need to weep and laugh and hold her just to be sure this person, this Lisa, really was who she claimed to be.

"The lander, the ambush. I thought you had died… "

"Almost," Lisa said. "But the Iaens… ." Her hand went to her face. "The Iaens healed me."

Of course. The Gift, already at work.

Tor became aware of Lisa's companion.

Shu Qingchun.

"What the hell are you doing here?" Tor said. "Why aren't you locked up in the brig?"

"I'm sorry. I know you don't want to see me or listen to what I have to tell you" Shu said. "But this, this is too important –"

"Too damn right, I don't want to hear it. I want you out of here. Now."

"Tor, please listen –"

"Get out."

Stricken, Shu turned to Lisa, who nodded. Shu made as if to make a last protest, then left.

"Why are you working with him, Lisa? The man's a traitor. He sent us into that ambush."

"He denies that he knew what was going to happen. He was acting under orders from the Council."

"And you believe him?"

"I don't know what to believe, but we have to work with him. He's been reassigned to a Senior Advisor Post."

Tor uttered a rueful, humourless chuckle. "They're rewarding him?"

"Tor, none of that is important right now."

"Not important –"

"Please shut up and let me speak."

Tor was stung into silence. Lisa looked as shocked as he was. "I… I'm sorry, Sir, I didn't mean to… "

"It's okay. You're right. I'm listening."

Tor slumped down to sit on the edge of the bunk and waited.

Lisa took a breath before she spoke. "President Ammal, she's... The World President died in the night. A stroke... "

Dead? The President was dead? Tor grappled with the word and the vast rolling cloud of ramifications it dragged in its wake. He fought the dullness woven about him by the drugs.

"Can we keep her body alive, until we get the Iaen Gift back to Earth?" A moment of lucidity.

"No, I'm sorry. She requested that if she died, she must not be resurrected, on religious grounds."

How could she make such a request ahead of her death? She knew about the Gift in advance of Tor's mission, that's how. They all did, the whole Council. And turning down a second chance at life, no, that didn't sound like Ammal. The woman was a force of nature. She was strong, alive with energy, never resting... This wasn't right.

"A stroke?"

"A shock to us all. She seemed so healthy." Lisa shrugged. "Everyone is trying to come to terms with her death."

I bet they are, Tor mused. Are you part of this, Lisa? You have reason to be. You are, after all, another miracle wrought by the Iaens. You must be so grateful for your own second chance. Can I trust you? Is everyone around me involved in this... this what? Conspiracy?

"Mr President," Lisa said and offered her hand.

"What?" Another reality unfolded in Tor's mind with drug-blurred slowness. Christ. Nightmare upon nightmare. *He* was President now.

Tor ignored Lisa's gesture and forced himself to return her stare. He saw hope, fear. "Leave me," Tor said.

"Sir?"

"Go, please. I need a moment to think." The walls were closing in. This new reality was yet another voice that babbled in his ear. He needed peace, silence, solitude.

"Of course, Mr President." There was hurt in her voice. "Comm me when you need me."

Tor didn't see her go. He was on the bunk, head in hands. He heard the door hiss open then shut.

That was the moment when the beast pacing behind the bars of self-justification and shock finally tore its way out. That was the moment he broke. He collapsed onto his bunk wracked with tremors and fighting for breath as he tried to comprehend the magnitude of his crime and the sheer crushing weight of responsibility that had suddenly crashed onto his shoulders.

He reached for his pills. There was a bottle of scotch in the cabin too. He would need that as well.

Hours later, days perhaps, he was dragged from his stupor by Lisa's voice on the comm.

"Yes, Mr President, may I speak with you for –"

"Come in, come in. Please."

When the door slid open, Tor glimpsed two huge security guards, members of the presidential protection squad; volunteers who were genetically modified from muscle-bound hunks into monstrous, barely human, killing machines.

Lisa entered and this time Tor hugged her. "I'm sorry I was rude. You didn't deserve that. You have no idea how good it is to see you and know you're alive and well and that we're working together again."

"I feel the same, Mr President." She sat down on one of the cabin's two couches.

Tor took the other couch and tried to push away the need to swallow another handful of trancs.

"We have to work on your speech. You'll need to speak to the media the moment we land."

"Yes, I suppose I do," Tor said. "But first, Lisa, how much do you know, about Ia and what happened there?"

"I don't remember much after boarding the lander to fly to the war zone. I only know what I've been told."

"And what's that?"

"You voted for an attack."

"I ordered it." Why was he able to talk so openly about

it in her presence? Whatever the reason, it was a relief. "Katherina Molale? What do you know about her?"

"She was killed. She was in Tal territory, without authorisation. There was nothing anyone could have done for her. It was her choice."

The party line, fed to Lisa and, apparently, swallowed whole.

"What about you?" Tor asked her. "Are you fully recovered?"

"Just as Shu was. Like I said don't remember much, one moment I was in the lander, the next I was lying on the floor in the *Kissinger's* cargo hold with a handful of others. I must have been dragged from the wreckage of the lander. I was disorientated, nauseated but alive and," her hand went to her face as it had the last time she was here, "healed."

"Others?"

"Marines who were badly wounded in the crash and the firefight." Healed and back on duty. Humankind had an army of immortals now. Humankind was unstoppable.

"The rest of the casualties could not be recovered and even if they had been... they were too far gone for the Iaen Gift. Even that has its limits."

The Gift, that was what it was called now. A sweet name for such a profound and world-changing reality.

"I'm sorry, Tor, we've lost some old friends."

"Yes, we did." Tor realised that he had not even begun to mourn for the rest of the diplomatic party.

Lisa was suddenly all business. "The surviving journos would like a statement."

"I'm not sure what to tell them."

Lisa reached across to place her hand on his. "Tor, you did what was right. You destroyed the Iaens' enemy. Tell the journo pack that the Tal were a threat to the Alliance and to Earth –"

Except they weren't. Katherina had uncovered the truth that it was the Iaens who were the invader, Ia was the Tal home world.

"–You regret the breach our action has brought

between humankind and its allies, but hope that it will be healed in time. You wish the Alliance no ill-will and hope to open negotiations with them at the earliest opportunity."

"I... I... can't." God, it was hard to breathe. The pills were taking a long time to take effect this time. He needed a drink. He craved the numbing fogginess that particular narcotic-alcohol cocktail would bring. "I've broken the Second Alliance Protocol, humankind has been expelled... Christ... "

Lisa's arm was about his shoulders now. She held him tightly and murmured that it would be all right. He needed to be strong. Humankind would be looking to him for leadership and reassurance. "You're popular. With the people. With the Council. Even ArchTheocrat LeMay has sent a message of support."

Oh yes, LeMay, another fly in the ointment. He was the charismatic and, in Tor's opinion, power-hungry leader of the global Theocracy, a multi-faith, but mainly Christian, religious movement that was gaining a lot of traction back on Earth.

"And remember Eva," Lisa said. "Thanks to the Iaens, you're going to have your daughter back."

Yes, Eva. He calmed a little, then the narcotic bliss descended and his fears and guilt were bulldozed back behind those unassailable chemical walls.

*

Tor was on the move before the sun had left the horizon. He wound his way through the Garden to the cliffs then descended to the beach and headed north along the coast. He took nothing with him because he intended to scavenge food and drink on the move. He refreshed himself with a wash in the sea. His bath was brief, the ocean was too dangerous for him to linger in its dizzyingly cold embrace. Many of the beach-hugging plants bore edible fruit, which were dense and juicy enough to ease his hunger and quench his thirst.

The low sun scattered splinters of light onto the restless waves. Pterosaurs wheeled overhead then swept down to skim for food. Tor glimpsed huge bodies break the surface. Tentacles lashed at the water then struck out to knock an unwary pterosaur out of the sky and into the ocean where it thrashed and flailed then disappeared into the belly of a dark serpentine carnivore.

He kept a wary eye on the path ahead. He heeded the voices, the connections and instincts. This version of himself was not someone he recognised. He was physically hard, fit, strong and, tired as that old phrase had become, at one with the planet that was his home.

The salted breeze was clean and harsh. Spray washed his face. He moved closer to the waves. Molluscs were scattered over the wet sand. He harvested them and pressed his thumbnail into the gap between their clenched shells to prise them apart and suck out their soft bodies.

Scrubby bunches of prickle fruit clung tenaciously to the sand. Tor carefully reached into one of them to harvest its fruit, avoiding the tendrils that were the tripwires for the plants' vicious mobile branches. Each branch was lined with thorns big enough to tear flesh down to the bone. Mi's flora was as dangerous as its fauna. He had the scars to prove that this was an acquired skill. The fist-sized, dark purple fruit lay at the plant's heart. It was soft but dense enough not to squash in his grip. He gently curled his hand about the fruit, and twisted, slowly, until he felt it snap from its branch. Not daring to breathe, he drew it out a centimetre at a time.

The effort was worth it. He sat down on the sand and bit into the sweet, juicy flesh. He revelled in the dizziness of a sugar rush.

He also sensed oncoming danger. A monster, racing towards the shore, the smell of his flesh in its nostrils. It surged through the deep water, accelerating towards the moment it would explode out of the waves and onto the sand, immense jaws crashing shut in a detonation of broken bones and spattered blood. Tor's bones and blood.

Not yet, though. He still had five minutes or so. He

would know when it was time to move back from the shoreline. It would be in the moments before the beast's hunger grew so strong and overwhelming he could no longer find him*self* in the storm of instinct that would flood his consciousness. He sat for a while longer, brushed by the shadows of the wheeling pterosaurs, washed by the spray, warmed by the sun that ascended over the restless waters. He would sit and relish every mouthful of the fruit. He would feel the touch of the planet. He would let the edges blur between his self and the lifeforce of Mi. Every second here was known and enjoyed, every moment wrung dry of all sensation and joy it contained.

He may misjudge his escape, or stumble and fall. The creature might have a longer leap then he anticipated. That was the future. That was a thousand moments away, a thousand sparks ignited in the waves by the sun, a thousand kisses of spray, a thousand droplets of the prickle fruit's lifeblood on his tongue and in his throat.

Now.

He pushed himself up onto his feet and jogged towards the cliffs.

A vast, red-black energy slammed into him. His mouth watered, not from the fruit but the prospect of flesh. His own flesh. He moved faster. He slipped, went down on one knee, thrust himself forwards, energised now by natural prey fear.

He heard a roar of disturbed water, a howl of joyous hunger. He grabbed at the cliff face and stumbled to a halt then turned to see a titanic, mottled body crash onto the beach. Tentacles ignited great detonations of sand. He saw its mouth, wide and curtained with countless needle teeth. He saw its eyes, handfuls of them. Soulless and formless scattered about its head.

A tentacle tip slashed the air a few millimetres from his face. Its underside was lined with a hundred backward facing spines. Tor gagged on its fishy stench. He darted right and ran along the cliff base. The creature thrashed and twisted then lumped across the beach in pursuit.

Propelled by paddles it moved startlingly fast. The weight of it thudded against the ground as it lifted and fell.

Tor ran, carefully. He kept the cliff face close on his right. He leapt rocks and driftwood. He swerved to avoid strands of oily, treacherously slippery seaweed. He glanced back. The creature was still coming, but slowing now, exhausted by its own clumsiness on land. He couldn't stop yet. This was about endurance now.

Exhilarated by the chase, he laughed. This was living, here on the threshold of death.

A howl of frustration ripped through the rhythmic pulse of the sea. A pack of pterosaurs circling overhead scattered in panic. One last backward glance showed the predator's defeated slide back into the waves. For a moment, it was a dark shapeless mass in the shallow waters. Then it was gone.

Breathless, Tor doubled over and allowed himself a few gasping minutes to celebrate his victory. Then he continued his trek northwards. Surely he must have lost the Other by now, presuming that his doppelganger was still alive, of course, but he needed to be much further on to be sure.

*

The DNA tracker has him, but I don't. I'm already exhausted, not only from the trek round the borders of the garden in which I was almost killed last night, but also from the tension of simply staying alive on this planet. I am also disadvantaged by a backpack in which I carry food, water and a medikit.

The tracker picks up other life forms. Vague readings indicate living things, none of which seem that friendly in my brief experience of Mi. Real Tor has got a good start and is moving north, so I cut diagonally across the landscape, looking to head him off. The going is hard but it does mean that I avoid the garden, which is a lethal, amorphous, riot of colour a few hundred metres to my left. The ground here is cracked and rocky, strewn with hillocks and dips which force me to climb and descend constantly. I can hear the distant roar and hiss of the sea over which I flew during my lander's brutally rough descent. Now that had been a terrifying experience. Strapped into an empty spacecraft, at the mercy of its artificial brain.

The rock itself is covered in primitive looking moss and succulents. Their flowers are delicate and unutterably beautiful. They also make the undulating landscape treacherously slippery. There are rough pathways that wind between the hillocks, but they are diversions. If I am to catch up with Real Tor today I have to struggle on in as straight a line as I can.

Small mammals scuttle by, presumably too tiny to be harmful but I'm not taking any chances. Birds flit from rock to rock. Larger flying creatures circle above me, born aloft by massive leathery wings. They resemble the pterosaurs of ancient Earth. Again, I am unsure if they are a threat or not.

Most disturbing are the voices. No words, just the sense that someone is whispering nonsense into my ear, but never there when I spin about to look. There are feelings, too, of being watched and yet by nothing specific, and from no particular direction. It is as if the whole planet is aware of me and observes my progress intently. There are moments when the sensation intensifies. There are moments when I experience the hunger and fear of others. I begin to regret crushing the tiny plants underfoot as I clamber over the hillocks and low crags then half slide into the small valleys and ravines between them. I am convinced that they feel pain.

There is more here than mere landscape and non-sentient life.

The sun is still low, but the air is warming up. There is a breeze, light and chill. I sense that it should be cherished because there will be little in the way of comfort once that huge sun reaches its zenith. For now, two washed-out looking moons hover in the opposite side of the sky. One has an entire pole-to-pole hemisphere caved in, as if battered by an immense fist. Debris from the wound is strung out across the sky, held in place by the moon's gravity.

The waves become louder with every hard-won step. The air is a meld of perfumes; sweet scent from immense flowers in the garden, and the salty ozone tang of the sea. I clamber up to the peak of a hillock, a little higher than the others. It gives me a good view of the remaining landscape that separates myself from the edge of the cliff.

I scan my surroundings and, for the first time since I arrived, take in the beauty of this place. My joy is short-lived.

A clutch of those stick-thin bipeds are gathered around a large rock about two hundred metres away. Some of them crawl over the rock's flanks, or recline on its flat top, others move around at its base. They don't seem to be aware of me at the moment but it's going to be difficult to work my way past them. I check that my burner is safe in its holster. I don't want to use it anymore. I've slashed and burned enough of the planet's life already.

I also check the DNA scanner. Real Tor is almost a mile away and moving fast. He seems to be down on the beach, which is probably better-going than this. His route takes us in the direction of a jagged mountain range. Their slopes are purpled by the misty morning sunlight, their foothills shrouded in forest.

Okay, I move off to my right, intending to take a long arc around the stick men, hopefully far enough away for them to remain unaware of my presence. Then I'll climb down onto the beach. I tread as carefully and quietly as I am able. There are techniques, available in my counterfeit memories of the childhood I never had. The young Tor Danielson once trekked through forests and built camps with others of his age. He learned stealth, but right now, every boot fall sounds like a hammer-blow.

The stick men are following me.

The realisation is stark and so powerful it almost stops me in my tracks. I want to look over my shoulder but resist the temptation. I need all my focus and energy to keep going. That sensation of hunger is back, that craving for raw flesh and blood. I'm seeing the hunt through their senses. Not visually, or hearing myself, but the feelings, the instincts and cravings.

I press on. The sun is higher, the temperature rising. I force myself up the next slope. I want to rest when I get to the top but can't afford the luxury. It's there that I turn and look back and see them scuttering over the hillocks and outcrops, disappearing into the shadows then out again. Two of them collide in their eagerness to get to me and a vicious squabble breaks out. There seems to be little team spirit among their ranks.

The others, however, are gaining on me.

I slither down yet another slope then break into a tired jog. They are wearing me down and they know it. I wind my way between two hillocks, where it's cooler and damp. The moss on the rock faces is slimy and wet. Things squirm through them. I don't touch. Tiny creatures are usually the ones that burrow into flesh. I'm thankful for my gloves and boots. I feel vulnerable down here in this dank narrow cut. I've made a mistake taking this route. I lose my grip as my boot slips on the slimy ground.

I unholster the burner.

Then the natural passageway ends and there is a plain spread out in front of me and extending all the way to that forest by the look of it. The cliffs are a few hundred metres to my left. I can sprint across the flat then a climb down to the beach. It doesn't look as if it's too high. On the other hand I might trap myself, but I have little choice.

A moment.

Okay.

Now.

I run. A backwards glance reveals the stick-men gathered on the edge of the flat. The sight of them standing there disturbs me. Why don't they give chase? They seem afraid. Last night they pursued me across that other plain to the lander, so it is not that they are nervous of open spaces.

They are afraid of *this* open space.

Which means that I should be as well.

My sudden fear drives me into a faster run. I feel anticipatory dread.

The ground explodes in front of me. A great gout of soil boils into a choking brown mushroom cloud. Plants and rocks are thrown upward and outwards. A huge section some fifty metres across is ripped open like a giant trapdoor.

Something dark and titanic emerges, indistinct in the sudden fog of dust and debris. It moves fast. Another eruption to my right. Another. That hunger is back but this one unfocussed, this one primitive and without any semblance of thought.

I fire at the monster ahead of me. I see legs, a huge bloated body. Pincer-like jaws. It recoils but is too vast and dense for the weapon to do more than burn flesh. It is unsure though, which gives me a chance to run past it. Another bounds in from my right. It is armoured, gleaming and metallic despite its subterranean existence. Beetle, bear, worm, Christ, I don't know, it is too fast and big and dark and too full of violent hunger for me to stop and study its physiognomy. I run and fire blindly. Heat cuts through the choking murk.

Another of the beasts appears in a shower of muck and stones ahead and to my left. It is huge, almost as big as the lander. I veer right, because that takes me into its blind spot. How do I know that? Who cares? Right. Go right. Now, left and on towards the cliffs. Fast. Faster.

Legs emerge from the fog, clawed, chitinous and thorned. I weave again because this new monster is still trying to locate me. I feel it. I *know* it. That blind groping confusion, that desperation and hungry rage steers me through the lumbering, monstrous army. It fills my head and my instinct is to fight it, to grope back and restore my identity, but I resist. I need to *be* them. My life depends on it.

A further eruption of soil to my right and a massive surge of living hell leaps at me from the depths. A claw snaps about my ankle and then the ground slams into my back and I can't breathe. My mouth is filled with dirt, my eyes sting and burn. I'm moving, bumping over the rough surface. The monster has me and is dragging me to itself. Something vast and dark looms over me.

Then I'm wrenched up into the air, dangled by my trapped ankle, free leg waving and kicking. Blood rushes to my brain. The world is inverted and confusing.

I still have the burner.

I can still –

Wait.

Not yet.

A head, under my own. Pincers, jaws, open, serrated edges.

Wait.

Opening, wider.

A hole at their base, a tongue, tentacle, Christ knows what unwinds out its blackness.

Close.

Closer.

Now. Now. *Now.*

I fire into the thing's mouth and scream in terror and awful exhilaration as I do so. I am thrown backwards through a blizzard of ichor and tissue clots. Then I crash onto the ground once more. I roll, scramble to my feet and run and run. My fear is not only my own. I feel their dread of me. I feel the pain of the one I have wounded.

I feel the planet's disgust.

The cliff, a drop, steep but not sheer. I scramble and slide in a storm of rocks and stones. Faster and faster. I claw into the cliff face, I dig with my heels but I'm no longer in control. The beach races towards me then I see sky, sea, sand. I am battered and punched then hurled onto my belly.

All I can hear are the waves and my own breath. Every part of me hurts. I am broken, every bone splintered and useless. I will die here. Fresh meat for the creatures who inhabit this beautiful hell hole of a planet. Please let me be dead before the first claw or fang rips me open.

I lift my head. I can feel everything, so my back isn't broken. I can move fingers, hands, arms, legs. I can roll over and slowly, stiffly, sit up. I can see, hear, and smell the briny perfume of the sea.

My skin is caked with filth. My mouth filled with the taste of earth.

I struggle to my feet and shuffle to the edge of the waves then kneel to wash away the dirt. I realise that I still hold the burner in my fist. Echoes of the monster's pain still shudder through me. It no longer matters that I wounded, possibly killed it, to save myself. I caused it agony. I destroyed a living thing. A being. I haul myself to my feet then throw the weapon out and into the heaving waters.

*

It was deafening. Tor staggered and clamped his hands over his ears in an instinctive, but vain, attempt to block out the mind noise. It was an explosion, a roar, a howling maelstrom of need and drive.

The Other must have strayed onto a burrower trap. Christ, he would never survive that. Even Tor, with his highly attuned connection to Mi, would be hard-pressed to scramble out of that one alive.

He hesitated, head pounding with the rhythm of the burrowers' hunger, and wrestled the compulsion to go back and attempt a rescue. The Other was not a monster. He was an intruder, unwanted and unwelcome, but he was a human being who did not deserve the kind of death he faced. Or, more probably, had endured already. And if so, then Tor was free of him and could return to the Garden and let the newly-ignited memories burn out and fade once more. On the other hand, if he was alive, how could he simply walk away?

Hadn't Tor spent most of his life in the service of humankind?

47

Yes, he had, refugee camps, politics, the Peace Legion, but he didn't want to remember any of it. He wanted only the *now*.

Fuck it.

Tor turned and sprinted back along the beach. The raging madness of the burrowers' attack was a red fire in his head. It fogged his vision and overwhelmed all other voices and sensations. He was barely aware of the distance, of his own labouring heartbeat and breath. The sea crashed and foamed unnoticed. He had to find the Other.

He saw the cloud of soil and dust that hung above the cliffs and rolled down onto the shoreline. Burrowers, made indistinct by the fog, milled back and forth along the cliff edge; huge, lumbering but capable of sudden spurts of violent speed. One of them reared and bellowed in frustration.

A figure stumbled from the gritty mist. Human, unsteady. His hair was wet and rat-tailed. His overall was drenched. He had been in the sea. Was he insane? The ocean was even more lethal than the land.

It was the Other.

His eyes were wide and he was gasping for breath. He looked battered and shocked.

"We need to get out of here," Tor shouted to him.

He felt suddenly awkward. This man was *him*. The way he stood, walked, breathed and swallowed. His voice, every feature, tic and mannerism. The person who looked back at him through the Other's eyes was Tor Danielson and yet a separate, distinct soul. He was not a reflection, it was deeper than that. The man facing him on this alien beach was no quirk of light and glass. He was real. There was connection and disconnect. He felt judged, which was ridiculous, nonetheless he recoiled from the sensation that he was confronted by a better version of himself. Someone who had taken a different fork in the road that led either to perdition or salvation.

Again, untrue. This replica, this changeling, was never on Ia. This thing was never Eva's father.

Tor walked on and did not look back. He heard the Other's footfalls in the sand. He heard his laboured breathing. You would have done exactly as I did, he told him silently. You are me. You would have given that assent and brought down the fires of hell on the Tal. You would have…

Fuck, now more of it was breaking through.

The reason for that terrible moment on Ia.

Eva…

Why wasn't Annika with Eva?

Suddenly he was walking down the *Kissinger* lander's ramp into a storm of vid lights and journos, a pack of them, hungry for a statement, for misstep, for something, anything with which to fill their mediaprogs and vidcasts.

"Mr President. Mr President." The prefix to every shouted question. A title that still felt as if it applied to someone else because the inevitable Pavlovian conditioning had not yet set in.

He moved slowly, carefully. The numbness provided by the pills he had swallowed prior to Earthfall might be peace-giving and reassuring, but it also locked him inside the cumbersome machine that was his body. He struggled to remember where the controls were. When he found and mastered them, he discovered that they were sluggish and unresponsive.

Lisa was at his right hand. He could feel her tension, and readiness to grab him and support him if he stumbled. Shu was on his left, just as tense but for a different reason. He was a traitor. So why were the press calling to him as well, treating him like Tor's co-hero?

"Is it true that you were brought back from the dead, Mr Qingchun? Is it true you offered yourself up, that you sacrificed yourself for humankind?"

A familiar figure waited at the bottom of the ramp. A woman in an expensive coat. Annika. Smiling. Happy to see him. His wife. She shouldn't be here. She despised him. She shouldn't smile or hold out her hand for him like that. Confused, too disorientated to do anything else, Tor went to her and they embraced and he buried his face in the faux fur that she wore and breathed in her perfume and found sanctuary there.

A tap on his shoulder. Lisa urging him to take to the podium.

His speech. Yes. The words he had to say.

He had burned them into his memory, terrified that the drugs would slur his words and turn him into a mumbling idiot. He needed to retrieve them now and repeat them, clearly, confidently, presidentially.

Lisa stepped up to the microphone. "Ladies, gentleman and all of the Press, I give you the President of Earth and Governor of all Her Colonies."

Applause. Some cheering.

"Thank you for this reception," Tor heard himself say. He glanced at Annika who had replaced Shu on his left. "I am deeply touched. As I stand before you now as your new President, I wish with all my heart that it was not in these circumstances. President Amman was a political giant. Her wisdom, compassion and friendship will be sorely missed. Stepping into this role, I now know how it feels to stand on the shoulders of giants and will do my best to carry on the work she has begun.

"However, with sadness comes joy. The Iaen-human alliance has never been stronger. Our friends on Ia, humankind, and the Alliance of Planets, have all been spared the horror of invasion and interstellar war by the brave actions of our armed forces and the decisiveness and moral courage of the World Council."

This was bullshit. This was untrue, pernicious, propaganda. Don't listen to me, Tor yelled from behind the curtain of self-regarding lies, it wasn't like that at all. But his voice was silent and that other voice, automated by fear of discovery and the ruin of his family, droned on to deliver more crowd-pleasing nonsense.

"The Iaens have rewarded us with countless gifts. Technology, science and medicine will all benefit beyond measure from the Iaens' bounty." No mention of *the* Gift, not yet. There were obviously rumours, but that was how it needed to remain until the Gift's introduction, use and control could be worked out. "As for our breach with the Alliance, I will seek to meet with their representatives and negotiate a new treaty at the earliest opportunity. I am sure they will be open to talks. This unfortunate rift in our relationship is both heartbreaking and harmful to all concerned and I am confident that this wound can be healed. Thank you. I will take no questions because, right now, I need to get to the hospital and to my daughter."

The pack ignored his closing statement and shouted "Mr President, Mr President," until he and Annika were safely inside the armoured Presidential runner and racing through the bright-lit streets of Stockholm towards the Karolinska University Hospital.

"Thank you," he said and turned to Annika. "I'm sorry… "

Her hand was limp in his, her face blank. "Annika? What the hell? Anni –"

"Mr President, Tor." Lisa on the opposite seat. She leaned forward to take Tor's hand in hers. "I'm sorry, but this isn't Annika."

"What? I don't understand?" His disorientation was complete. He wanted it all to stop. He wanted to shout, to scream and rage and break something.

"I'm sorry. I thought you had been briefed on this."

He probably had, most of the voyage home was blurred and confusing. Details were slippery, dreamlike. He understood then that he had to get a grip. He had to discard artificial wellbeing and face up to the immense responsibilities of his new office. He had to fight down his guilt and grief and do the job.

"This is a replica," Lisa waved towards the now unconscious Annika. "A proto from CellTech's seeder tanks."

"Why… what the hell is happening?"

"She was formed to be the loving wife welcoming her husband home, but nothing more. She will go back into the tank for re-cycling. She isn't real. She wasn't given much of a personality or self-awareness."

"It sounds bloody cruel to me."

"It's all about image, Mr President. The First Family has to be perfect. No fault lines, especially now we need the support and cooperation of LeMay's Theocracy. They are all about family values and morality. The real Annika's at the hospital. She knows you're on your way. The Iaen screen has been delivered and is ready. It was thought best if you were there when… when it's used."

Tor mumbled something about the illegality of replicating living people, but Lisa assured him that sometimes rules needed to be re-interpreted for the common good. Even in his narcotic haze, Tor could hear the discomfort in Lisa's voice. Like him, she was spewing out the party line and choking back the truth.

The runner took them to a hospital back entrance, away from the journos and the public. There were guards everywhere, heavily-armed, genetically-modified monsters. Tor hurried inside. Doctors and senior nurses waited for him. He smiled the brief, sad smiles expected of a president with a sick daughter then followed them through bright-lit, gleaming corridors that had been cleared of patients, visitors and staff in the name of security, to the room where Annika and Eva waited.

And here was the scene he had seen so many times in those tense, painful holo-comms between the hospital and the *Kissinger*. Annika, seated by the bed. Eva, pale and corpse-like, connected to the machineries that kept her body alive via a web of tubes and wires.

Annika didn't seem aware that Tor had come in until he placed a hand on her shoulder. She flinched then looked up and it was obvious that she didn't want his touch or to speak to him, or even be in his presence.

Before, when Tor returned from diplomatic missions, haggard, tired and homesick, he would be engulfed in her arms the moment he crossed the threshold to their home. No more. His affair with Katherina Molale had torn apart their marriage. The damage seemed irreparable.

"There isn't much time," Tor said and suddenly the medication-haze was gone and everything came into brutally sharp focus.

"What are you talking about?" Annika's voice sounded dry and unused.

"Bring it in," Tor ordered. "And then I want everyone out of this room except Lisa Kavanagh. And shut the door behind you. We need some privacy in here."

The Iaen screen, brought back from Ia by the *Kissinger*, was wheeled through the door. It was about two metres in height, the same in width. Its surface was black and featureless. The room then emptied and door closed as Tor had requested.

"What the hell is that?" Annika said. "What are you doing? Get out, Tor. Leave us alone."

"Annika, please, listen, this is for our daughter."

"Get out."

"I am going to help her."

"Get out, for God's sake –"

"Annika," Lisa said. "Trust me, if you can't trust Tor, please."

Annika looked conflicted now. "What are you going to do?"

"Something good for Eva. I promise," Lisa said.

"You need to move away from the bed," Tor said. "For a moment."

Annika looked to Lisa who nodded. She slowly got to her feet. It was obviously an agony for her to move from her daughter, as if she feared that Eva might fall into the dark the moment she released her hand. She allowed Lisa to draw her gently to the corner of the room.

"Annika, I'm saving our daughter," Tor said. God, he hoped that was what was about to happen. He loved Eva with every fibre of his being. Her imminent death was an agony to his soul.

A pulse began in his temples. A migraine threatened.

The Iaen screen flared into life. Shapes swirled and slithered through each other like snakes formed of clouds. A human couple danced out of the swirling murk. Something scuttled over the screen's inner surface. Clouds roiled. Lightning flickered. Vast, violent waves reared from the chaos and hurled themselves against the glass.

Tor clenched his fists against the pain and nausea. He heard Lisa weep. He saw Annika drop to her knees, arms wrapped about her abdomen.

Then the madness in the screen coalesced into the silhouette of a rough-hewn humanoid, almost two metres in height. A moment later, it stepped out of the screen and into the room. Annika uttered a cry of shock. Tor recognised it as an Iaen in physical form. Expressionless and silent, the Iaen crossed to the bed and slid its arms under Eva's shoulders.

Annika's shock turned to anger. "What are you doing? Leave her alone. *Leave her alone.*" She made to rush the Iaen but Tor grabbed her and held her back. He felt her struggle in his arms then subside into weeping. He wanted to cry himself. He wanted to collapse and give in to the hot agonies that tore through every part of him.

The Iaen lifted Eva from her bed. Tubes and wires tore free. Her head lolled back. Tor's headache intensified into rhythmic hammer blows that sent shockwaves through his nervous system. Annika screamed in protest as the Iaen carried Eva towards the screen's madness of cloud and lightning. He stood before it for a moment with Eva in his arms, then pushed her against the screen with a quick, rough action that made it look as if he was smashing her against its surface. It was an abomination, a horror show.

The shapes in the glass erupted into a frenzy. Cloud opened and boiled and fire bled out and huge, unnameable creatures writhed and slithered and scuttered and there was music and dancing couples spinning wildly through the inferno –

A gasp.

A cough.

Eva?

Eva.

The screen went blank. Eva struggled in the Iaen's arms. Tor watched her pull feebly at the pipe that ran up into her nose and gag on the one down her throat. Tor slammed the call button. Where was the doctor? Why were there no medical staff?

The Iaen laid Eva back on her bed. Annika pushed past him, snatched her daughter to herself and held her tightly and wept and laughed. The Iaen, meanwhile, stepped back to the screen and dissolved into its roiling surface. It took no more than a handful of seconds for it to disappear. The screen darkened once more. No one, other than Tor, appeared to have noticed the Iaen's departure.

A moment later the room was invaded by shouting doctors and nurses. Tor slipped out, quietly. He needed privacy. He needed to be alone. He needed to allow it to overwhelm him and to break him under its onslaught. He needed to be alive and human again, if only for a moment.

The panic of guilt returned. It would never go away.

They couldn't know.

Annika and Eva must never know the price of resurrection.

*

An almost imperceptible chill cut through the warmth. There was a slight increase in wind speed. An unease in the air and in the vast, combined consciousness that shared Tor's own. A storm was on its way. Distant, but racing over the ocean towards them at terrifying speed.

Tor looked back to see that the Other was still a few metres behind him. He looked tired, still shaken from his encounter with the burrowers, no doubt. Tor turned his attention to the cliff face. They were exposed out here, on the beach. There was no sanctuary to be found on the cliff tops either. The burrowers' plains stretched for many miles between the edge of the Garden and that forest which troubled Tor so much.

The wind strengthened. The temperature dropped a little further. The sea's horizon was thickened by a dense band of cobalt-coloured cloud. Tor's search for a refuge moved from urgent to desperate. He steered towards the cliffs, which were fissured with cracks. Most were too narrow to provide shelter, or too unstable looking, littered as they were with debris from rockfalls. Tor was beginning to despair of finding anything suitable and was resigned to huddling at the base of the cliff face and hoping for the best.

There, a huge crack. He scrambled over to its mouth and peered inside. Yes, high enough, dry-looking. No debris.

"This way," he called out, then without looking to see if the Other had heard him, "Hurry up."

He listened for signs of life, opened his mind and reached inside the opening. The cave seemed to be empty, but he needed to be sure. Stickmen tended to crawl into cracks and crevices to ride out the storms. This would be an ideal hiding place for them.

Nothing. No whisper, no snarl, no trace of fear or hunger that wasn't his own. Okay, he would take a chance. He stepped inside. The place was narrow and went back perhaps four metres or so. It was large enough to accommodate two human beings.

Tor sat down on the cold rocky floor, grateful for the rest. A few minutes later the Other joined him, taking his place against the opposite wall.

"Why the panic?" the Other said. His own voice. God, *his own* voice.

"Storm coming."

"I thought I felt a change in the air."

Felt? It didn't take long for Mi to crawl into your head and make itself known did it, False Tor.

"When it's over, you need to go back to your ship and leave."

"I will, but not until I get what I want from you."

The hiss and roar of the waves outside grew louder. The light dimmed.

"Whatever it is, you can't have it."

"I want the truth. I want you to tell me what happened on Ia."

"You know. You're me –"

"What really happened. *What* happened. I only have the knowledge, the facts. I don't understand *why*."

"I don't remember." Tor knew that he could if he wanted

to. "It's too… Since you arrived I've remembered too much already. Why the hell can't you leave me alone?"

"It has to be faced –"

"Oh, I've faced it all right. I've let it rip my heart out. Believe me, Tor Danielson what, the Second, Third, you don't want to *know*." Tor closed his eyes. There was noise outside now and he welcomed it. Conversation was becoming difficult, thank God. Animals were calling to one another, a final warning to find refuge. Tor let the babble fill his head. He opened his mind to the electric song of the approaching storm.

"I need to know why." The Other said. "I'm a simulacrum. I know you, but I don't *feel* the way you feel. I need to know why you did what you did on Ia. I have to understand."

"You know what I did. What more do you need?"

"Tor Danielson has to stand trial."

"Before whom?"

"The Alliance of Planets." The Other paused. "There's been shifts, changes, since you disappeared."

"Why am I not shocked?"

The first gust of wind screamed in from the ocean. Suddenly the conversation Tor didn't want was impossible anyway. He saw the Other flinch away as a deafening peal of thunder followed hard on the heels of a dazzling blue-white flash of lightning. Another flash, and everything in the cave was thrown into stark monochrome, an instant of chalk white walls and skin and grotesquely elongated shadow. Then all was lost in a barrage of boiling waves, screeching wind and a maniacal dance of thunder and lightning. The sea slammed itself towards the cliffs, building into great black walls of water hurled up the beach towards the cave mouth. Each time it was wrenched back to regroup for another assault.

There was music in the storm. Timpani, dissonance, broken by the occasional piercing beauty of the hurricane as it probed the cracks and crevices of the cliffs.

Music…

Tor had always found Sibelius's Violin Concerto problematic, even now, as he sat beside Annika in the Great Hall of the Humanity One Space Station and watched their daughter Eva weave solo after solo from bow and string.

Despite its size and grandiose architecture, the hall was an intimate venue. There were hanging gardens, a waterfall and rock pool filled with exotic fish. Its white walls curved up towards a huge glass dome through which the titanic blue-white curve of the Earth could be seen.

The audience, a hundred or so of the most beautiful, richest and powerful, were the only ones who could afford, or were entitled, to be here. Millions more watched on vid-link and could only dream of being allowed a ticket. Money wasn't the only key to unlocking this treasure chest. Tor took no pleasure in his right to be here. Yes, his joy at seeing his daughter alive and feted, was immeasurable, but he hated the exclusivity of it all.

Eva's playing was sublime, but the piece itself continued to irritate. It was the way in which the violin solos seemed separated from the orchestral moments that held the work together. It was almost as if those passages were simply there as adhesive and not as momentous moments of their own.

But wasn't that *his* life now?

Annika, the orchestra, supportive, in the background. Tor, the soloist, hero of the Iaen Emergency. The adored People's President. That's what the media called him.

Tor was not so sure of Annika's feelings towards him. She stared straight ahead and never so much as glanced at him. He deserved it, he knew. He had betrayed her with another woman. He tried to hold her hand, but she snatched it away. Her rejection of him was discreet but definite.

Heroism and popularity ended when he was alone with her.

"It will take time," she had said a few hours after Eva's miraculous recovery. He stood in their apartment a few metres from his wife yet hearing her words as if from a hundred miles away. "Tor. I love you for what you've done for Eva, of course I do, but I can't... I can't just break through this wall. I know that makes me cruel and ungrateful, and for that I'm sorry."

Tor didn't answer. Words eluded him. Whether because of his hurt or the drugs, he couldn't tell. The latter certainly shielded him from the full force of the rejection, but rising through the haze was the need to feel her in his arms; comfort and reassurance when he deserved none.

Even for the miracle up there on the stage, Eva, momentarily alone in the spotlight, the orchestra reduced to formless shadow behind her. She glowed, a beautiful, willowy, creature of grace and consummate skill. Eva, once clinically dead and now alive, because of the greatest of the gifts the Iaens had bestowed on humankind. Her music, once silenced, soared and burned again. It tore at the heart. It was bright and then dark. It was immaculate and beautiful.

Another solo rose from the rolling ocean of sound to reach beyond the walls of the hall and out into infinity. Tor swallowed an emotion so strong it had pierced the chemical shield that protected his seared and tortured conscience.

The Sibelius concerto finished to a standing ovation, flowers for the leading musicians and Eva again, lost in the bliss of a triumphant performance. Tor's commer buzzed in his ear.

"Meeting Room Three Mr President." It was Shu, now Senior Advisor to the new Secretary of Interplanetary Affairs. "It's urgent, sir."

Shu wielded a lot of power since his return. He had influence. He was listened to. He was also a traitor, a schemer. Tor had wanted to sack him, but, unlike Shu, Tor did not have power or influence.

Tor Danielson was a puppet who dangled on the Council's strings. And he loathed himself because of it.

He made his way from his seat to the aisle then, a bodyguard at each shoulder, walked quickly out of the hall. A tube runner waited beyond the grand doors at the hall's transport node to whisk him the one-point-five kilometres to the central administration section. Humanity Station was the current seat of humankind's government. Created because it was felt that to choose any place on the globe would defeat the object of having a neutral, all-inclusive Council. Better that the Council were based above the Earth.

There were five people waiting in the conference room. All resplendent in their concert evening wear. Vahini Khatri, Secretary for Defence, Andries Brouwer, Tor's replacement as Secretary for Interplanetary Affairs, Natalia Yegorova, Secretary of Global Affairs, and Shu Qingchun and Lisa Kavanagh, who Tor had retained as his Press Officer. She was the only person he trusted.

"It's time to discuss the Iaen Gift," Natalia said. No welcome or comment on Eva's performance, no, it was straight to business. "There have been leaks, conspiracy theories, the media are beating at our door."

"What's known?" Tor, voice calmed by antidepressants. "What are these conspiracy theorists saying?"

"Mostly the truth," Natalia answered. "That the Iaens have given us something wonderful and that the government is holding it back from the populace."

"So far, the media have toed the line and kept the lid shut," Lisa said.

Katherina wouldn't have, Tor knew. She would have blown it wide open.

"Plenty of hints and glimpses," Lisa continued. "But none of them has revealed everything yet."

"*Yet*," Andries said. "How long can you keep them on a leash, Lisa?"

"A few days. A lot of editors and owners are already screaming about freedom of the press."

"Now there's irony." Andries offered one of his trademark wry smiles. "When an editor's freedom only extends as far as the owner's views."

"We can't keep it hidden any longer, Mr President." No smile from Natalia Yegorova, wry or otherwise.

"The moment we reveal the truth, the world will go mad," Vahini Khatri said. "There will be anarchy."

"Exactly." Natalia said. "But we have an idea." She glanced at Andries.

This was how it was. No one had referred to Tor, no one asked his opinion or paid him any respect. His presence was required at these meetings but only as a figurehead, it seemed. He kept his anger at bay. He needed to be careful. There was a lot at stake, and it behoved him to toe the line. He knew that he was weak. He felt that he had no choice.

"It's risky," Andries said. "But maintains control over its use and renders any cries of conspiracy theory redundant." He nodded to Shu who made to activate the holo-pad, but hesitated.

"If I may Mr Secretary, Mr President," Shu said. "I need to voice my concern that this plan has the potential to be disastrous."

Tor was startled by Shu's sudden swerve from the ranks.

Natalia was on her feet. She leaned across the table, her posture one of threat. Shu held her stare. When she spoke there was venom in her voice. "I don't think this is the time for –"

"Let him speak," Tor said.

A moment of what felt like shocked silence at his presumptuousness.

"Go on," he said to Shu.

"Thank you Mr President."

"Don't thank me. You weren't so averse to taking chances on Ia," Tor couldn't help himself. The moment he said the words he felt petty and childish, shifting the blame for his own heinous act. Also, his personal dislike of Shu had surfaced, another display of weakness. Why was he even here, still in post? He had been party to the whole deception, Tor was certain of it, but then hadn't everyone else in this room, this nest of vipers who ran all humankind. "But, I'd like to hear your objection to whatever scheme Andreis has cooked up."

Shu's obvious discomfort at being in the room with Tor seemed to intensify. "I understand your hostility towards me, Mr President, but I only ever act in the best interests of humankind and take my responsibilities as an advisor seriously. In this case I am convinced that the risk attached to the plan is too great."

"Show me what you have in mind," Tor said. He was tired. His head ached.

The holo flickered into life to show the inside of what looked like a large church or cathedral. The congregation was enormous. Every pew and seat were taken. The aisle was crammed with standing congregants. The light was warm yellow. Tor could almost see the heat generated by all those bodies crammed together within those vast, high walls. The vid scanned the building to reveal grand, domed ceilings decorated with ancient, beautiful religious murals.

"This is the Duomo in Florence," Shu said. "Three days ago."

The anticipation in the church was palpable, even through the holo. It rose to fever pitch when a figure in clerical vestments ascended to the pulpit. He was tall, broad, imposing. His jaw was square, his features rugged. He possessed the looks and presence of a vid-star. Tor recognised him as ArchTheocrat LeMay, head of the Theocracy that now encompassed all the world's religions and who, Tor knew, was gathering thousands of new followers every day. A huge cheer went up, applause, chants of "God's chosen, God's chosen," resounded around the cathedral, until LeMay raised his arms then slowly lowered them. The gesture brought the volume down to silence.

"My friends." Deep, booming voice, filled with authority melded with warmth. He was speaking to every person in that building, every vid-watcher, personally. A clever trick. A well-honed skill. "I come to you as a representative of the Many-Named God to bring news of a miracle." Pause for effect. "The miracle of the Iaens, God's own messengers, through whom, I believe, He has shown himself to humankind." Amens rose from the congregation. Tor was unnerved by the mob-mindlessness of that response. "They have led us out of our fearful association with the Alliance of Planets, a godless relationship with the non-human, with the warlike and brutal, with species who practice Satanic rituals, who devour their own children if born disabled or misshapen. Monstrous creatures who claim the name of civilisation. The Iaens have set us free of their influence."

Amen.

"He's not above good old-fashioned xenophobia and fearmongering," Lisa said quietly. Andreis turned on her sharply. A signal for her to keep her opinions to herself.

"The Iaens have bestowed many gifts on humankind," LeMay continued. "They have given us technologies that will enable us to bring both civilisation and the Word of God to the furthest reaches of the galaxy."

Amen. Amen. *Amen.*

He waited until there was silence. Total, electric silence.

"I am telling you, my friends, the Iaens are angels."

Yes. Yes.

"God's own messengers. Divine, holy and terrible."

Yes. *Yes.* Amen, amen, amenamenamen.

"I believe this with all my heart. Do you?"

Oh yes, yes we do.

"It is they who appeared to Ezekial as the wheels, it is they who cleansed Isaiah's lips with a burning coal. It is they who ministered to Elijah and made known the Saviour's birth to the shepherds. The Iaens are the angels of God and they have come to guide us to the next stage of our great and sacred Alliance with the one true, Many-Named God, the God of humankind. I tell you –"

The holo was disconnected at a signal from Andries.

"You get the picture," he said, "This man attracts audiences of thousands. On that day, there were twice the number of worshippers gathered outside the Duomo than were inside. His sermons are broadcast across Earth and out to the colonies. They are received and believed because LeMay offers old certainties to people confused and frightened by contact with the alien and unknown, by the pace of technology and human expansion across the galaxy. We have gone from environmental catastrophe and global war to interstellar travel and extra-terrestrial alliances in a shockingly short time. We have encountered alien civilisations that range from the sublime and god-like to the demonic and hellish. LeMay represents continuity, reassurance and a god that people can trust and believe will protect them."

"He is also encouraging the belief that the Iaens are Divine beings, Angels," Tor said.

"Exactly."

"So, what is this plan?"

"We hand the Gift over to LeMay, and he administers it as a miraculous reward for the faithful."

"And lose control of it completely?" Lisa this time.

"LeMay is loyal to the Council," Natalia said. "He encourages unquestioning faith in the government. He uses that story about Christ, the one that ends with 'Render unto Caesar what is Caesar's' to keep his followers in line. By handing him the Gift, we disassociate it from the government and turn it into a gift from God."

"But," Vahini said. "We maintain control of it with regards to the military and those in positions of responsibility."

And the rich, Tor added spitefully. He didn't voice his cynicism.

"Are you sure of his loyalty?" Tor said. Again that sense of disconnection. "You're handing control of the most wondrous and devastating tool humankind has ever possessed to a cult leader?"

"You can hardly describe that," Andries waved towards the now frozen vid image, "as a cult. The Theocracy is no mere handful of religious crackpots. It is huge and powerful, and it is the largest organisation on Earth."

"Is that supposed to reassure us?" Tor said.

"It certainly doesn't reassure me," Shu said in an

unexpected show of solidarity with Tor. He took off the spectacles he wore purely as a fashion item and cleaned them with a cloth he produced from his tunic pocket. A nervous gesture.

"LeMay will do as we ask," Natalia said. "He wants to reach out to our colonies. Raising the money for that kind of venture will take him a long time, unless we provide the funds and logistics for his mission."

"We buy him," Andreis said.

"This is too dangerous –"

"Think about it, Mr President." Never had the title been so loaded with sarcasm. "LeMay's following will increase a thousandfold. All that adulation, power or whatever it is that he craves will be more than even an egotist like him can handle. But, the focus will be away from us. The responsibility for administering the Gift will be his and no one will see it as fair. It will tear the Theocracy to pieces in the end and that is when the Council will, reluctantly, step in and bring it under tight control. To do that now would be seen as the elite keeping the Gift to themselves, being forced to take that control if the Theocracy collapses will be seen as salvation."

"Too dangerous," Tor said and realised that he was repeating himself. His mind was slippery, his thoughts fluid and impossible to distil into sentences. A deep breath, a moment to construct his statement. "I will not sanction this."

"You will," Vahini said. She sounded almost amused by his protestations. To her he was a fish on a hook, wriggling and struggling for freedom that would never be granted.

"Mr President, may I speak with you alone?" Andreis said.

Tor glanced at the others and saw open hostility in the faces of Vahini and Natalia. Concern in both Lisa and Shu's expressions. Odd that Shu should be sympathetic. Hypocritical, in fact. No, no, he should let that go. Shu was taking the role of ally. Tor needed all the friends he could get, even if they were treacherous and dangerous.

Tor nodded to Andreis.

The others left the room. It was suddenly quiet and empty.

"Tor," Andreis said quietly. That quietness was dangerous. "You are in no position to oppose this."

Tor waited.

"Your family don't know the truth, do they? How do you think Annika and Eva would feel if they discovered that an entire race was destroyed for them? And that race was not the invader but the original inhabitant of Ia. What would it do to your daughter if she found out that her healing, that her life, was bought by genocide? What would it do to her professional reputation? What is she, fifteen now? On the cusp of a glittering musical career. And your wife? That left-wing firebrand you met and fell in love with all those years ago. It would be the end of her, you know that don't you. Your family would be shamed, shunned and destroyed."

"Fuck you," Tor said. The insult spilled from his mouth before he could prevent it. It made him feel weak and crass.

"No, Tor, you're the one who is fucked."

"You're implicated in this."

"Really? It's you who found out that the Tal were the victims here. Through your former lover who you also sacrificed at the altar of selfish need to heal your daughter at all costs. Katherina Molale is another dirty little secret of yours Tor. A scandal that has, so far, never leaked out into public. The People's President is not the angel the *people* think he is."

Tor no longer gave a damn about his own reputation, but he loved Annika and Eva and could not endure their destruction.

"So, Mr President, I assume we can proceed with Operation Miracle?"

No gesture or word of affirmation was necessary. Andreis left the room to set the Council's plan into motion. Tor took a moment to compose himself then set off to join Annika at the reception being held in Eva's honour.

*

He's gone. He's out there somewhere, in a storm that would have had the four horsemen of the apocalypse running for shelter. I don't remember him leaving. I must have fallen asleep. I don't understand why he is running? I only want to talk to him. I only want to *know*.

All I can do is huddle in this cave and sit the storm out. Christ, I have memories of visits to some wild planets, borrowed memories, inherited and yet as real as if I had actually been there, but this is more vicious than any of them. It's almost as black as night, the cloud so dense little sunlight can pierce it. The lightning is constant and brutal, I peer out of the cave mouth and see it slice down into the sea which erupts and boils to steam, and onto the beach to kick up fountains of molten glass. The wind is hurricane force and laced with enormous hailstones that look as if they could pummel you to death.

And Real Tor is out there. Not sheltering or lying low. The DNA scanner shows him moving northwards. How the hell is he alive?

I shrink back into the cave. I can afford to wait out the storm. He isn't going to get far in this weather.

My skin prickles with static electricity. The combined jet roar of the wind and sea and the titanic hammer blows of thunder batter my ears. Worse, is the way it tunnels into my mind. The way the unseen forces of the tempest flood my senses and white out all the connections that were forming between my consciousness and Mi's id. I feel lonely, frightened, like a primitive ape huddled in the dark, trying to comprehend the fury outside. It is as if the storm is a living thing, screaming and pounding my soul. I am sure that it will reach into my shelter, wrench me out to pull me to pieces and cast my broken parts into oblivion.

The severed link leaves me lonely, vulnerable.

All I can do, is crouch and flinch and cower and wait for it to end.

*

This was insanity. This was a death wish. The storm beat at him as he staggered along the beach. Hail battered his head and shoulders. The gale screeched in his ears, tore at his hair, and froze his bruised and battered flesh. Lightning scorched the air in sudden waves of blistering heat as it blasted into the sand and turned the shoreline into a minefield. Impenetrable cobalt-coloured cloud roiled overhead, terrifying in its restlessness. The blackened sea was lifted into three-metre walls of water that exploded into volcanoes of sand and foam as they slammed into the ground. Water swirled about Tor's feet, ice cold and alive with currents that tried to wrench him off balance. And all the time, an artillery barrage of thunder shook the universe to its foundations.

He pressed on because he had to. He could not remain in that cave with the Other. His very presence had unpeeled yet more unwanted memories. They were a vast weight that crushed him to the dust. He had thought them gone. He had been set free by the shimmering electric blaze of connections forged on this world. Now his past was spreading into the light like a poisonous black ooze. The guilt had returned. The guilt over the sin he had fought so hard to atone for as a Peace Legionnaire.

And there lay a whole other raft of painful recollections, of disease, disasters and desperate rescue missions. Of men, women and children made homeless by flood, landslide and quakes, ravaged by bullets, shells and burners, or by the alien viruses encountered on the planets humankind had colonised.

Tor no longer wanted anything to do with any part of humankind. He would not tell some fake version of himself how he felt or why he had committed that crime on Ia. He would not submit to some scan of his neural pathways and emotions and memories. He would not leave the surface of this planet.

The beach narrowed ahead of him and twenty or so

metres further on looked to be completely flooded. Each wave smashed at the cliff face making it impassable.

He had to climb to the cliff top as quickly as he could. There was a rockfall at the edge of the narrow beach. The water here was deeper and made for an icy wade as he headed for the fall.

Once there, he clawed his way upwards. He clung to the rocks as the hail scourged his back. The wind tugged then shoved at him. The waves boiled beneath him. Lightning strobed the world into jerky, stuttering unreality. He felt the concussion of each thunderclap vibrate through every hand and foothold.

Pull, push, up. Up.

He dragged cold, wet air down his throat. He felt his heart thud hammer-like in his chest. He felt his strength ebb away. It would be easy now to let go and fall into peace and nothingness. It would be easy to let the storm take him.

Instead, he dragged himself to the next set of hand and footholds. And the next and the next. He drove through his exhaustion. He would live. He would escape the Other by outrunning him until he was worn down and defeated.

And would he be?

The Other was himself. The Other was Tor Danielson who was unwilling to abandon this climb. The Other was Tor Danielson who did not give up.

He crushed the thought. He climbed.

Until.

He reached the cliff top. A sodden flatness under his groping hand.

The rock fall shuddered. There was a crashing sound, louder than the din of the waves and the storm. Tor felt the rocks shift under his feet then tumble away. The fall was collapsing. The wild sea had probably swept away its base. The cause didn't matter. Tor needed to get up onto the cliff top. Now. He groped frantically for something to grip and found a root, wet, slippery but solid. He clenched it tightly in his wet, freezing hands and hauled himself upwards.

More rocks rolled away. For a moment, he hung in midair, feet scrabbling at the cliff face. His shoulders were a mass of pain. His hands burned as the root slid through his palms. He dug his toes into the cracks and flaws in the rough wall and shoved himself upwards. He yelled with effort, drenched, battered, desperate. He hauled and strained and suddenly his chest was level with the cliff edge. He kicked and dug with his feet. The root seemed to become more slippery with every second.

Stomach against the edge, bent double, crawling.

The sodden mush of vegetation on the cliff top was a bed for him to lie on. He buried his cheek in the slimy storm-rotted plants. He remained there for a timeless moment, his exhaustion complete and all consuming. He may have passed-out because suddenly the storm had eased into a steady, driving rain and the clouds had lightened to grey. The gale was now a stiff, icy breeze.

He shivered but didn't care about the cold. He had survived the storm and for a while he once again found himself living the moment. Each victory savoured.

At last he hauled himself back onto his feet. The weakening storm meant that the Other would resume his pursuit soon if he had not done so already. Tor surveyed his surroundings. He was on the borders of the burrowers' plain, not far from the forest. Beyond lay the foothills of the mountain range. He was at the northern edge of his explored territory. He had avoided the forest until now, but it seemed as if he needed to enter and face whatever lay at its dark heart. Perhaps the Other would baulk at following him there. Perhaps he would finally be rid of him.

It seemed that he had no choice.

*

The storm quiets and, although unpleasant, I can leave the cave and walk along the beach without fear of being struck by lightning or swept away by the angry sea. It is cold and my overall is soon drenched from the rain. That does little to lighten my mood. Real Tor is still on the move. It is hard to believe that he survived the storm, more than that, that he kept moving even when it was at its cataclysmic peak.

The wind and rain quieten with startling suddenness, half-an-hour or so into my own trek. The dense cloud cover dissolves and the gold, evening sunlight breaks through. The sun is low. Two moons have risen and are still made pale and ghostlike out by the lingering daylight.

It's dangerously late to venture out, especially as I am now unarmed, but I cannot allow Real Tor to wander out of scanner range. My burner lies on the ocean floor. My wits and the burgeoning connection with the Mi id are my only protection. That connection has suffered during the storm. It was raw and vestigial anyway, but it is coming back. I need to learn how to use it, and quickly. Perhaps I should let the voices and sensations grow louder and stronger, instead of fighting them, which is my instinctive reaction to this invasion of my mind.

The sea is still agitated. The beach is strewn with detritus; weed and shellfish mainly, thrown ashore by the giant waves. Frighteningly big shapes break surface, tentacles writhe and thrash, as if stirred up by the storm. Some of them seem to be heading for the beach. I break into a jog. There is a rock fall a hundred metres further on. Its base is spread wide, part of its stony skirt reaches as far as the waves. I don't feel safe down here. But then, have I ever felt safe?

The rest in the cave has been good for me. I feel fit again. I've eaten and the food replenished me.

I feel the sea monsters. I hear their voices and know their terrors and hungers. I understand why I am hunted, why I am hated and rejected. I am an invader, an intruder. I don't belong here. I use tools and weapons from outside to kill and destroy. I may have discarded the burner, but I still have the scanner. I need it. The thing is vital. It is my only way of finding Tor. Humankind's colonies are depending on me to do so, but the scanner is a machine and the artificial is not welcome here.

A loud bellow brings me to a halt, and I turn back to see a huge shape slither from the water. A serpent by the look of it. The thing is immense. Its dark, gleaming body seems never-ending as it slides out of the waves. Another joins it, thrashing and writhing onto the beach then erupting into a snake-like, sideways slither over the rough sand.

Now I run. The waves crash on my left, the cliffs rear high on my right. The serpents are at my heels and gaining on me. The rock fall I saw, only reaches to halfway up the cliff face. It will do. Anything will do right now. I surge towards it, feeling as if my lungs will burst. The ground shudders as the great beasts slither in pursuit. The beach is uneven, littered with storm debris and large stones. I leap and stumble and am in terror of tripping and falling. I am certain I can feel the heat of the nearest serpent's breath on the back of my neck.

I throw myself at the lower boulders of the fall and scramble upwards. Every limb aches. I am grazed and bruised but feel none of it. When I reach the top, I twist round and try to shuffle myself into a secure position. There are two serpents. One has already reached the base of the fall, about six metres below me. The thing slides between the stones and works its way upwards. I see its dead, white eyes and open jaws, which are lined with ranks of needle teeth.

Worse, I can feel its desperate hunger. It is a drive that is almost madness. It has to reach me. It has to feed. There is nothing else in its mind.

I grab at a rock, the largest I can hold in one hand, then hurl it at the nearest of the beasts. The throw is accurate and the rock bounces off the thing's snout. It recoils and unleashes an angry-sounding bellow. The other serpent joins in. The noise is terrifying.

It resumes its ascent. I scrabble at the loose shale and rocks then throw again. And again. The first misses. The second smacks into the creature's jaw. Another recoil. Another bellow. I lift a larger rock, heavy and large enough to require two hands, and to do a lot of damage, if

I can score a direct hit. There is only one way to improve my chances of that.

The serpent has to be close enough to be an unmissable target.

So, I wait.

The creature's impulses and single-minded urge flood into my mind. It has no plan, no strategy or guile. It sees food and, for the next few seconds, that is the entire meaning of its existence.

Oh God, the thing is monstrous. It is quick and strong and unstoppable. But still I crouch and wait. Until I can smell its cold, fishy perfume and once more feel the heat of its rotten breath. Until the world is swallowed by the stinking cave of its mouth and the yellowed cage bars of its fangs.

I stand, my legs wracked with pain as they drive me upright. I raise the rock above my head with both hands and feel horribly vulnerable, as if I am offering myself to the oncoming beast. It moves its head, exposes a white, formless eye.

Not yet. Closer. Closer.

Close enough for it to strike.

Now.

I lob the rock with all my remaining strength and watch it arc with unnatural slowness down towards the serpent. It ignores the oncoming missile. It has no understanding or concern. It sees only food. The rock bounces against its right eye. There is an eruption of a black liquid that sprays out and over me as the monster shakes its head, presumably from pain. It bellows and howls. I shrink back, waiting for the agony-crazed attack, but the monster seems confused by its pain. It writhes and twists into huge black-shining knots. The other serpent swerves back and forth in a desperate attempt not to be crushed by its pain-maddened twin then, finally gives up and slithers back down towards the beach.

The rock fall is suddenly alive with a surging mass of armoured, crab-like creatures, each about the size of my palm. They are heavy and fast and scuttle from every nook, every tiny crevice, a torrent of them that pours down the cliff on either side of me and over my feet. They fall upon the serpent and within seconds great holes have been torn into its flesh which give entrance to armies of the invertebrates. I'm trapped here on the rock fall and can do nothing except watch the great creature devoured from the inside. It continues to twist and thrash, long after its outer skin ripples as the hordes of crab-things tunnel through its body.

I hope that they will be satiated and not turn on me when they've finished. But why would they? They were hiding in the rock fall all the time and had not shown themselves until there was easy meat available.

It's dark when I judge it safe to make a descent. The way down is illuminated by my head lamp. I make my way past the meaty ruins of the serpent. Stretches of gleaming, white skeleton have been exposed by the crab-creatures. Loose stone rolls from under my feet and more than once, I fall on my backside. I hear scuttling sounds that probably belong to those stick men, drawn by the huge feast now laid out on the rock fall. Like most carnivores, they no doubt prefer an easy meal to the effort involved in hunting.

Back on the beach, I resume my pursuit of Real Tor. He still shows up on the DNA sensor. North and inland. I pass several rock falls each providing a way up to the clifftop, but I'm reluctant to go back up there until I'm closer to the forest where I'm now certain he has gone to ground. I also want to avoid the plain where those underground horrors lived.

I need to catch up with Real Tor soon, because the Colony Federation ship that brought me here cannot remain in orbit indefinitely. I will give myself one more day then return to the lander, empty-handed. It would be a failure, but if that is the case I will make the best of it and face the Alliance with what I have.

There is plenty of light despite it being night. The two moons that dominate the sky paint the shoreline silver. Splinters of moonshine dance on the waves and throw the landscapes of the cliff face into stark contrasts of harsh light and deep shadow. The rocks are further lit by some species of fungus. Swarms of fist-sized fireflies add their light to the general nighttime illumination. The water, too, is streaked with swirls of rainbow-hued phosphorescence, especially along the crests of the waves.

The beach is dangerous. More of the sea creatures could surge out of the water to snatch me in their jaws. There might be stick men lurking in the shadows at the base of the cliffs. There's nothing I can do but walk and hope that I'm unnoticed by the local wildlife. I can feel them, sense them. There doesn't seem to be any immediate threat, but I've learned that things can change very quickly here on Mi.

I decide to climb the next rock fall I find. Surely, I'm close to the forest now.

A quick glance at the sensor reveals that I'm nearer to Tor than I was an hour ago. Which means that he is making slow progress. He isn't resting however. He's still moving.

*

The lichen and moss that clothed the rocky surface of this, the northern edge of the burrowers' plain had been turned into muddy green mush by the storm, which meant that the going was slippery. Exhausted by his ordeal in the storm, Tor slid and stumbled over the unreliable landscape towards the forest. The trees were merged together into an amorphous blur, made impenetrable by night. For all its mysteries and threat, the dark of the forest was interpreted as a place of sanctuary by Tor's weary mind, even though he sensed that it was far from a safe place.

It possessed a presence that was almost sentient. The electric brightness of Mi's id intensified with every step and seemed to vindicate Tor's theory that the forest and others like it were nodes in the planet's life force, repeater stations if you like.

Close now he began to pick up the voices of the forest's inhabitants. The place teemed with life. The alienness of some of that life was disturbing. He would be hard pressed to track or predict their movements and intent. The voices were loud in his head. So much so that Tor was forced to shut out the noise altogether. The only way he could achieve that was by letting more memories seep into his conscious mind.

He entered the forest's borderlands then pressed on towards its heart. This was his last hope of throwing off his pursuer. He would try to lose the Other in the vast maze of trees and undergrowth, and in the mind-chaos of the forest's denizens.

He might also die in here.

So be it. He would rather face his end here than leave this planet.

The forest floor was lit by beams of moonlight that forced their way through the canopy. The trees seemed to be a collection of huge, thick-trunked deciduous species. Many of their muscular lower branches were less than two metres from the ground and a constant hazard. The floor was yielding and springy, the undergrowth, dense. Bracken-like plants lashed at Tor's legs as he walked. Water dripped from the upper branches as cold, heavy drops that thudded onto Tor's scalp and shoulders. It was Mi's own version of water torture. A thousand heavy but painless blows, slowly driving the victim mad.

Each footstep was important, the entire focus of his strength and effort. He could barely stand, let alone walk, but he wasn't going to stop. The vague plan of losing his scent in the blazing sensory maelstrom that lay at the core of this place had become a need to get there. He couldn't remember when or how the imperative had changed. His head was too full of colour and noise.

Tor tripped on some broken bough concealed in the undergrowth and fell against the trunk of a tree. He pressed his cheek against the rough bark and felt the warmth of the plant's life force. It calmed him. Exhausted by the storm and by the rigours of the trek, he sat down to rest on the soft ground in the bracken. The place thrummed with the music of predators and prey, but Tor felt safe while he was close to the tree. It was as if the forest knew that he needed to rest for a while and guarded him.

Tor closed his eyes and tried to fight a new raft of unwelcome memories that pushed through his exhaustion to plague him as they had since the Other had come to this planet. This time, however, he felt as if they had been drawn from his subconscious by the forest itself. It was as though the vast network of roots that laced the earth beneath had spread tiny filaments into his sub-conscious and were drawing out the toxic remembrances that infected it.

He was in his apartments on Humanity Station, A few hours on from the meeting, and drinking steadily in an effort to numb the shock of Andreis' blackmail. It was, he knew, a double-edged sword. Any revelation about what actually happened on Ia would reflect back not only on Tor, but on the Council. After all, they had authorised the illegal military operation already in progress against the Tal when Tor had arrived on the planet. They had also supported his decision to order that final tight nuke assault.

He was not the only one balancing on a tightrope over the abyss.

The anti-depressants helped. They unhooked his mind from the guilt and reduced the outside world to a movie in which he was an uninvested bit player merely plying his craft. The medication was, however, losing its effectiveness. The dose had increased twice already and exceeded the recommended maximum. He shouldn't be drinking as well, but he didn't care.

He contemplated an overdose, not for the first time since his return from Ia. He would escape into the darkness and it would be over for him, but it would destroy Eva. And Annika, despite her coolness towards him. He couldn't do that to them.

So, he sat and drank and let the wretchedness unfold inside him as it had done a thousand times already.

The door slid open.

"Tor?"

It was Annika. She wore a robe and nightdress and looked pale and tired. Her hair was dishevelled by sleep. But, for the first time, in as long he could remember, there was no hostility in her eyes. She crossed to the drinks cabinet and poured herself a red wine then sat down in the armchair facing Tor's own. She was beautiful as only a middle-aged woman can be, self-contained, assured, knowing. He loved her, didn't he? It was hard to untangle his thoughts.

"What is it, Tor?" she said. There was none of that ice in her voice that he had become accustomed to.

"What do you mean?" Thank God he was drunk. It provided an excuse for his slurred speech and drug-induced lethargy.

"Don't be a fool. I know you well enough to sense that there is something seriously wrong." Annika paused to stare at her wine glass. "Is it Katherina Molale?"

It was odd to hear her speak that name calmly, not wrapped in hate and used as a curse.

"Yes." Not a lie, because her murder was a bright thread that wove its way through the horror.

"Did you love her?"

A pause, then, because he could no longer lie, he said yes again. There was some release in that short, single-syllable word.

"Do you still love her?"

"I… I think I do." Confession. He tensed. The last time he had confessed there had been an apocalyptic fight. One from which they had not been able to recover.

"So, are you mourning her? Is that why you are depressed?" She raised a hand, as if to ward off any protest from her husband. "I know about the pills, though God knows what that quack has given you. Sometimes you're like a dead man walking. You're locked into yourself…" She shrugged. "Tell me, Tor, is this grief over Katherina?"

"Yes." That word again. This time, however, it was not big enough to cover his real grief. His sorrow for an entire race and for the sacrifice of his principles on the altar of personal gain.

"You did the right thing."

Tor was momentarily disorientated by her words. Did Annika know the truth? *The* truth?

Annika reached across, suddenly, and took his hand. "The Tal were invaders. They were a threat. Tor, you made the right choice."

She believed the lie. They all did. The Iaens, god-like and innocent, the Tal a poisonous aggressor bent on conquest. He had helped spread that lie himself. The truth was the reverse, starkly counter to the official version. The Iaens were the disease, the Tal were the infected. Or had Katherina been lying?

"Annika," he heard himself speak her name. He was going to tell her. He needed to tell her.

"Yes?"

No. Knowledge was dangerous.

"Enemy or not, lives were extinguished. Perhaps we could have talked to them… " Oh God, half-truths, self-pity. What else was he going to pile onto the barricade against the truth?

"Come to bed with me."

What?

Annika's hand closed about his. She stood. Tor was suddenly afraid, of his wife, of how this might end. He wanted her, he needed her, but there was peril in that want.

He followed her to their bedroom. There, his fear increased. He was unsure what frightened him. He lay down beside her and kissed her. At first she seemed uncertain, or was it reluctant? She drew back from him. He gently kissed her neck, her shoulders. He tasted her sweet soft skin, breathed in her scent. This should be home, this safe place in the dark, but it wasn't. It was okay. Tor took his time, forced himself to linger over each kiss, to *feel*. But there was nothing, only her flesh, only a human body, there was no connection, no desire.

Annika moved away and propped herself up on her elbow. "It's all right. I understand, Tor. We've been... I can't expect us to suddenly act as if nothing has happened." She paused. Then, "I loved you. From my very soul. That's why I was angry."

"Loved?"

"I don't know how I feel anymore."

"Are you still angry?"

"I don't know... Yes, I think I am."

"Do you love me?" Present tense. Did he really want to know?

A pause. No reply. No words and yet a thousand.

"I love *you*, Annika. I know it sounds trite and, it probably doesn't feel like it right now, but you are everything to me."

She sat up, her back to him. "I'm sorry, Tor. Whatever you call love wasn't strong or deep enough to prevent you from giving it to someone else."

"Do you still love me, Annika?" A last attempt. It sounded hopeless even as he asked the question.

"I don't think I do." She sounded as if she was crying.

Tor moved across the bed to hold her. She huddled more tightly into herself and away from him. He withdrew. The rejection speared deep and the wound bled into his guilt; a toxic, venomous mix. At that moment he no longer wanted to breathe or feel the rhythmic hammer-fall of his heart. He knelt on the bed behind her, knuckles pressed into the mattress, head bowed, defeated. Finished.

He felt Annika's hand on his back, soothing and warm. "I'm not going anywhere," she said. "I still care about you. I will stand by your side and hold your hand and I will be proud of you, because I am. God, Tor, you brought Eva back from the dead. How can I walk away from that? I don't even begin to know how to... how to *be*, with you, with myself, after experiencing the miracle you brought home to us. I will be your friend, your wife even, but, despite all that, I cannot be your lover. I'm sorry."

"So am I," Tor said then grabbed a robe and headed back into the lounge. He picked up a bottle of scotch on the way but did not bother with a tumbler.

Things snarled and snuffled in the nearby undergrowth. Some feeling of hunger broke through the din of Tor's memories and he caught a waft of his own smell; raw meat, sweat-tinged. He scrambled to his feet, ready to flee. Whatever was stalking him out there danced back in alarm at his sudden movement. He felt its fear, then caution. The predator slunk away. The connection stretched then snapped and it was gone.

The incident broke him out of his fugue. He needed to resume his journey through the forest. He had been foolish to rest. The Other was as dogged in his pursuit as Tor was in his retreat. It was logical to assume that the gap between them must have closed while he was resting.

Tor walked, difficult because, despite the bright silver moonglow, there was more darkness than light and that darkness was total. Tor waded through tall, dense bracken, was scratched by thorned bushes and sure that at any moment he would step into the embrace of some predator or other. There was also the possibility that some of the plants here were carnivorous. There was no way for him to avoid danger, other than listen to the noise in his head, but even that was too loud and shone too brightly for him to distinguish the malevolent from the harmless.

Not only that, the noise was further corrupted by the leak of memories from his sub-conscious and he was too tired to fight them.

"Mr President, Advisor Shu wishes to speak with you."

A voice on his commer, one of his security guards. Head spinning, nauseated, Tor sat up. He was in the lounge, on an armchair. It was still night on Humanity Station.

"What... What does he want?" Slurred, almost impossible to enunciate. It probably sounded like "Wadderewan?" He wanted to add *Tell him to go away* but stopped himself. As much as he disliked Shu, as angry as he was with the man, the advisor would not be waiting outside the Presidential suite at Christ-knew-what-hour if it wasn't urgent.

"Let him in." Tor made to stand but thought better of it. It felt as if sudden movement would empty his stomach over the expensively carpeted floor. Better to stay where he was and let it pass.

The door slid open and Shu entered. He looked ill. He was haggard, his eyes red-rimmed and he trembled. "My apologies Mr President, but I need to warn you about... Sir, Tor, you have to get off the Station."

"What the hell are you talking about?"

"I need to show you something."

"Sit down, here, have a drink." Tor offered him the half empty bottle. Shu cast about for a glass then changed his mind, as Tor had done, and put the neck to his lips. He took a long draft then screwed up his face as the sour heat hit.

"Now, slow down," Tor said, "and start at some point where this will make sense."

Another swig. Shu closed his eyes for a moment, then shuddered as the fiery brew once more found its mark. "Tor, I know you hate me. I betrayed you. You have no reason to trust me, but this time I'm trying to save you."

"From what?"

"You're a risk."

"I know that, but I'm dealing with it. I'm doing everything I can to protect Annika and Eva. That's the only reason I'm supporting that fucking insane plan to use LeMay –"

"Tor, stop. *They*, the Council, don't trust you, not broken like this. They think that you're on the verge of collapse. They can't control or predict what you might do if that happens." Shu took a breath. Then looked up to hold Tor's stare. "They're going to replace you."

"Replace... you mean impeachment –"

"No, you don't understand. They are going to kill you and –"

Kill him? "An assassination?"

"It will be quiet, discrete."

"And how do you make a World President disappear? Won't someone notice? I'm a popular fellow, don't you know. Humankind loves me." Tor chuckled at that. A dangerous, scotch-fuelled giggle.

"I've been given the task."

"You?"

"You are popular, which is why Tor Danielson is not going to disappear –"

"You are going to do this? You're supposed to kill me?"

"Yes." Shu appeared to shrink and crumple into the chair. "Yes, me. I am your assassin."

"You didn't do a great job of it last time."

"I did what I was ordered to do," Shu's expression darkened. "I didn't know what was going to happen. I swear. It worked, though, didn't it Mr President. The Council got what they wanted. The destruction of the Tal and the Iaen Gift."

Tor reached for the bottle. Shu handed it back to him.

"Keep talking," Tor said.

"I'm a Special Advisor, and this is my project. I'm trusted, because I did my job on Ia, and it was dirty work. I'm a hero, the man who sacrificed himself to bring the world the Iaen Gift. It was planned. I knew that Iaen was going to beat me to death, but I also knew that I was going to be resurrected. All to get your vote for war because we knew that you had a raw nerve, Tor, an Achilles heel. The Council was certain that the promise of a cure for Eva would be too hard to resist. I didn't know your lander was going to be ambushed and that you might be killed. I was acting under the orders –"

"Oh yes, the Nuremburg Defence."

"They promised me the world and, yes, I was ambitious and foolish enough to want it. So now, I'm the one who gets his hands dirty, which is why this new task has been passed on to me." He paused and asked for the bottle again with an outstretched hand. Tor shrugged and gave it to him.

Shu resumed speaking. "You are needed, Tor, but not *you*. The plan is to replace you with a proto from a seeder tank, a more reliable, balanced and pliable version. CellTech is in on this."

"Wait, stop. Isn't it illegal to create a proto of someone who is living? Protos are to be used solely for colony seeding."

"No one was arrested over the replica of Annika who met you at the docking port."

True. And she had been utterly convincing. For a moment he had believed that Annika had forgiven him.

"The law? Tor, they don't care. They're already growing a proto of you, here, on the Station." Shu was on his feet now, a vidpad in his hand. "Look, Tor, look at it. It's my project. My responsibility."

Tor did as Shu asked. The image of the screen was shaky, footage shot while the filmmaker moved through a room of gantries and metal ladders.

And tanks, each filled with murky fluid. Lumpen shapes floated in each one. The vid closed in on the nearest then moved along from tank-to-tank, until it stopped against one that contained a near-grown human figure. The figure twitched and twisted. Tor had seen this before, during official visits to CellTech facilities. The protos always made him uneasy. There was a wrongness to this god-playing.

The figure rolled over and floated close to the glass. It bumped against the tank's side and Tor saw its face.

His own face.

"Enough, turn it off." He realised that he was on his feet. He grabbed at the back of his chair. "How do I know this isn't a fake?"

"You don't," Shu said. "And you have no reason to trust me. But why am *I* here? Now, in the early hours, look at me, I'm a wreck. I'm terrified I will be found-out and made to disappear. No one will miss me, Tor. A few might mourn over whatever accident kills me, but I don't matter. So, why *me*? If this is a trick, why not send someone you trust and respect?"

The man had a point.

"So, why the sudden attack of conscience, Shu?"

"I sold myself on Ia because I believed, really believed, that humankind would be ennobled in some way by the Gift."

"Ennobled by betrayal and lies?"

Shu shrugged, as if unable to answer the question.

"Look at the way the Gift is to be passed into the hands of a holy snake-oil salesman," Shu said. "Turned into a cheap miracle to keep the mob happy and preoccupied while the Council consolidate their power and bring in legislation that will destroy the democratic process, because that's next Tor, be in no doubt. They've misstepped, however. The Theocracy is dangerous and the Council cannot see it. It's growing into a revolutionary movement. LeMay is charismatic, unstable and terrifying. His connection to the Iaens is deep and dark. Did you know that the Theocracy has funded the next batch of colony seeder expeditions; the *Drake*, the *Raleigh* and the *DaGama*?" Shu counted the starships off clumsily on his fingers. "Why did they do that? What is in it for them? Several senior military leaders are sympathetic to the Theocracy as well. They see LeMay as a strongman and the Council as weak. They want the Gift, but the Council is holding it back. Think of it, an army of immortals under their command, every casualty restored to fighting fitness in moments. What's next? A holy war, an interstellar crusade fought at the behest of ArchTheocrat LeMay?"

"What about Annika and Eva? What happens to them if I'm replaced?" The question seemed almost trivial compared to the epic horrors described by Shu.

"They won't know. They are important, but only because the Danielsons must be held up as an example of the perfect family, as role models. The Theocracy and its millions of god-fearing, self-righteous, adherents would baulk at the presidency being held by an adulterer who cannot keep his own marriage together. Also Eva's golden career as a musician will further win over the people. She is their darling. The product of a perfect marriage." Shu shifted in the chair, a sign of unease. "I'm well aware of the reality, Tor. I know that your marriage is not... that you are no longer close. But that fact alone makes the plan feasible. Annika lives her own separate life, only joining you for official duties, so she'll be unaware of any differences. And if she does detect anything off-kilter, well she can put that down to your drinking and pill-popping. The important thing is that she and Eva will be safe, in fact, they will be safer with your replica than they are with you."

"So, we're back to the quiet assassination."

"The plan. *My* plan, except that you are too important to lose. We need you."

"We?"

"Not everyone supports the Council or the Theocracy, especially out in the colonies. They feel threatened by LeMay, they are furious that we have been stupid enough to lose our membership of the Alliance. They feel weakened, and vulnerable. The colonies have allies who share their fears, in the government, a small group but we are growing, quietly, slowly. We will look to you for leadership when the time comes, but until then we have to hide you and keep you safe."

Tor realised that he was going along with this. "So, how do I get off the Station. I mean, I'm the President, in case you'd forgotten. I can't simply wander off into the sunset. Wherever I go, I have a security escort, a gaggle of advisors."

"It's my project, remember. I'm trusted to keep the Council's hands clean, so leave it to me, Tor. Be ready. It will happen sooner than you think."

*

I feel safe nearer the trees. I know I have no reason to feel that way. This forest is, no doubt, home to all manner of hungry beasts. But, there is something else here, something louder and brighter than the myriad sparks of animal, and vegetable, intelligence that swirl about the outer branches of my mind. The presence seems to be neither malevolent or benevolent. It *is*. One thing I am sure of, it knows I am here, picking my way carefully from tree to tree. It neither welcomes or resists my invasion of its leafy precincts.

There, the now familiar hungers and terrors. Over to my left, something huge and cumbersome. It's perception of this world seems confused. The thing is aware of me, my scent, the noise I'm making as I struggle deeper into the forest. It makes its slow, clumsy way towards me. I veer to the right to put extra distance between us and its mind fades from my own. Okay, this is how I stay alive. I watch and listen with my mind. I allow the connections to flare. I stop fighting. It's hard to do. Almost impossible to let go of what makes me Tor Danielson, but I do my best to let the voices in.

It's fully nighttime now, but a combination of slowly developing night vision and the brightness of the moons is enough to shed some light on my path. Real Tor is about a kilometre ahead of me. He is moving slowly, struggling every bit as much as I am. I pick up the pace. I move from tree to tree and stumble over their immense roots. Some of them undulate in the ground. I feel the thrum of their life force. I feel warmth rising from the earth where their roots interconnect.

There are roars and snarls, hisses and squeals from every direction around me. They grow louder. I mark their locations, their directions of travel. It is confusing, overwhelming. My head aches. There are too many living things stalking the night shadows. Some move through the branches above my head. Some flutter up from the undergrowth in a blaze of multicoloured lights.

Deeper and deeper. Now the trees themselves glow, limbs limned by pulses of green-white.

Deeper.

Until.

I am in Hell. I will never leave this forest. I can hear animals all around me, the plant life is venomous and vicious. I have cuts and scratches on my arms and face, my overalls are torn by the thorned tendrils that hang from the trees and lash at anything that passes. The lightest touch energises them into a blind grasp for prey.

I have been bitten and stung by innumerable insects. My imagination has distorted the glimpsed, but mostly unseen, predators into the denizens of nightmare.

The only thing by which I can navigate is the DNA scanner. Real Tor is perhaps half a kilometre ahead of me, but now moving slowly. The going will be hard for him as well, but he has given himself up to the planet, to the life that reaches out to touch the minds of anything that has one.

I want that too. I feel it flow through me, but cannot bear the shadowy malevolence of some of the life here. The din is a cacophony which overwhelms me. At first, I used it to find my way through the forest's many snares and traps. It was exhilarating to be guided by this sense. To know where danger lay long before it became a direct threat, but now there is too much. It crowds in and oozes from the trees, from the things that slither and scuttle and crawl.

I pass a huge centipede like creature, hanging limp from a noose of thorny tendrils. Its great body sags, legs stilled. As I pass I see that the tendrils have entered its body and are, no doubt, sucking it dry of its vital fluids.

The creature twitches and to my horror I realise that it is still alive. I feel pity for it, even though it is a monster that would have hunted me down and killed me.

The backpack straps dig into my shoulders. Its weight bears down on me. The DNA sensor is heavy now. I spin about at the slightest sound. I am going mad. There are voices that aren't voices but the cries of the non-sentient. I fight them off and it exhausts me.

Movement. Ahead. A huge thing that seems made from a twisted weave of branches rears out from the fungus and emits a piercing screech that resembles the cry of a misplayed violin. Then it collapses, falls apart into what looks like a pile of sticks and disappears into the fungus.

Further on. A place where nothing is still.

Tree trunks writhe and twist, their branches flex and reach out towards me. Deep booming sounds erupt from deep within their trunks. Gaps open and close like mouths. Things emerge and then slither back inside, snake like with mammalian heads, furred bodies. Huge serpentine beasts slither through the gaps between the trees seemingly unaware of me. The ground undulates and expands and contracts as if breathing.

There are voices here, hisses and sighs and low growls and jabbering gibbering nonsense and my name screamed from great distances.

I press on and clouds of iridescent flying creatures erupt from the dense, glowing plant life. They emit a huge sigh as they do so, human-like creatures scutter up the tree trunks, bodies translucent and giving sight of pulsing illuminated organs.

Vast things crash by. I see only legs, thin, haired. I stumble on.

Movement. Never ending movement.

I am now too exhausted to care and be afraid. My scanner tells me I am not far from Real Tor. He appears to be stationary. Resting? Wounded or dead? A huge tree blocks my path. For a moment it is ablaze with lights that dance over its trunk and lower branches. A deep rumble emanates from within its titanic trunk.

I walk towards it and, for a moment, a reddish light flares to reveal an immense crack in its trunk. It is the entrance to a cave-like space. I climb inside where it is warm. The place smells of wood and leaf mould and the walls and floor are soft and spongy. I sit and know that I am safe and, despite my fear and dread of this planet, find an odd peace.

I love this world.

And want to stay here.

Time passes but I have no idea how long. I think I slept.

Real Tor, I'm here to find him, not curl up in the wombs of sentient trees. I scramble out to resume my pursuit. It is still night, which means that I wasn't out for long, thank God. I check the sensor. Yes, a half kilometre or so away. Still not moving. I set off through a patch of long, thin grass-like leaves that wave as if on the seabed stirred by ocean currents. More of those glowing insects swarm from the plants ahead of me and cast multi-coloured illumination over the place. In those few moments the forest is like a gargantuan cathedral, the tree trunks immense columns that soar towards the moon-silvered sky.

Something human-sized, but wrong, somehow, emerges from behind a trunk about fifty metres ahead. Its movements are awkward yet at the same time, quick. There is an alertness about it. Its head snaps round and I feel its regard. It stands upright, torso thrust forward, legs jointed backwards. It looks like a small tree, long arms more branches than animal limbs. Head, a mass of twigs, leaves, or is that an illusion caused by the uncertain, silvery light. It has a horse-like muzzle. Too many eyes, scattered like a rash over the top of its snout.

Enemy. Kill. Kill it.

The thing's rage is like an electric shock. I stagger back, manage to remain on my feet.

Here it comes, rushing towards me in an easy, loping gait that clears the undergrowth with each step. I cast about for an escape route. There's too much darkness, a prison of trees, the drag of undergrowth. Its hatred engulfs me and I drop to my knees. I watch it come and try to prepare myself for the killing blow.

Come on, do it, quickly. Let's get this over with. For God's sake, *do it.*

Parasite. Bacteria. Virus.

I recognise it as another of the plant-like creatures I saw… when? Minutes ago? Hours?

It reaches out and its huge, long fingered hands close about my head. I smell the sweetness of new growth, the rot of leaf mould. The creature's grasp is gentle, but there is pain as its id floods my mind. It probes and searches. I can see nothing but hot white. I can hear nothing but a terrible buzzing sound that vibrates through my skull and sends electric shocks through my nerves.

It withdraws, suddenly, and straightens. I feel its confusion. The creature twists to go then seems to collapse into a tangle of branches and, in the muddle of light-and-shadow, appears to dissolve into the undergrowth. Another figure stands in its place. I recognise her despite the night-vagueness that hides her features.

I search my memories, trying to find her.

She holds out her hand.

The familiarity of her is like déjà vu. Elusive, buried deep in the cellars of my manufactured memory. Perhaps real, perhaps a dream.

I take her hand. Her skin is rough and somehow unformed. She is a replica, like me, yes, but also an approximation. I know her. Real Tor knows... *knew* her.

Real Tor loved her.

*

Eva?

There, in silhouette against the blaze of light that burned from the forest ahead. Tor stumbled to a halt in the crazed, swirling madness of light, smell and sound that not only assaulted his five physical senses but spiralled through his mind and brought with it disorientation and an odd meld of euphoria and fear. He couldn't remember when the forest changed from predator-rich darkness into this psychedelic glory.

"Eva? Wait, stay, wait... "

He set off in pursuit. It wasn't her, of course. It couldn't be her. The figure appearing and disappearing in the swirl of light was too young. How old would she be now? Twenty? Twenty-one. Not fifteen.

Reality no longer mattered. This Eva was real enough for him to have to get to her. He had to explain.

He was suddenly aware that he was the former World President, naked, stumbling through a forest that glowed and sang and threw sweet perfumes and vile stinks into the air and was impossible. It was surreal and ludicrous. It was absurd.

No, forget that, push it back to whatever black hole it oozed out of. He was no longer anything but Tor Danielson. Little remained of him but instinct, flesh and blood. His life was moments, each one filled with sights, sounds, smells and the ground he walked on and everything he touched. Every moment was dangerous and spent on the cliff-edge between life and death.

He drank water from the great leaves of ground plants. He ate the fruit, fungus and sea life he sensed, but was never certain, was edible. He picked grubs from fissures in the tree trunks from the stems of the spindly flowers. He was an animal.

As he struggled to follow the elusive Eva shape, Tor began to wonder why he was running. The Other was not trying to kill him. The Other merely wanted to talk to him. No, not talk, he wanted to tear open his soul and unleash the demons hidden inside. During his time on Mi, Tor had been able to forget, to lose himself and shed the monster he had become. But the walls were collapsing as he remembered more and more. He wanted it to stop. The breaches would heal if he was left alone. And that bastard would not leave him. Well, let him try to follow him here, to the heart of the forest, to whatever inner rings of Hell awaited there.

Shu's nocturnal visit, that was when Tor's life had first splintered into moments, each one to be savoured, each second with Eva, with Annika even when she was at his side, which was not often. The rift had widened quickly since that night of reconciliation and hard truths. Once the doors to their Presidential apartments on Humanity Station were closed, she would retire to her own rooms, obviously relieved to be away from her husband.

Knowing that, at any moment he would be gone, Tor had made time for Eva; coffee, conversation. She was busy, with school and with rehearsal as she prepared for her next concert. Eva was oblivious to the pain in her father's eyes, the tremor in his voice. She was too busy for anything but the briefest of conversations. Happy, focussed. Lost in her music. As it should be.

Only the drugs, with a side of scotch rocks, would alleviate the tension, which was steadily stretching him to a breaking point from which he knew he would not be able to recover. Two, three, five days passed. He attended meetings, made speeches for vidcast. All the time he felt the walls close in. He felt the fear and nervousness of the Council when he was in their presence. The threat was palpable, even through the haze of the anti-depressants. The business of those meetings, both formal and the ad hoc huddles in his office confused him. He was talked at or ignored. He understood only that he was supposed to be there to approve and authorise.

And all the time he awaited his supposed assassination, his exile or whatever it was that Shu had planned. He waited and it grew unbearable.

The moment came, eight days after Shu's visit, when the Gift was to be given to LeMay. The ArchTheocrat was invited up from Earth to Humanity Station, ostensibly to discuss a working partnership between the secular government and the Theocracy. The initial meeting was a meaningless exchange of platitudes and promises. Tor's hand was shaken and he shook others'. There was laughter and back-slapping. Lunch, which Tor picked at but could not swallow. More empty conversation. LeMay seemed adept at the art. He possessed charisma. His presence in a room was immense. His stare was intense and intimidating. There was steel behind the smile. Steel tempered with fire.

Then.

"We have something to show you, ArchTheocrat," said Andreis over the post lunch Port. "A gift in fact."

"And a responsibility," Vahini added.

"Intriguing," LeMay said.

The party that stepped aboard the specially reserved tube runner consisted of LeMay and his cabal of clerics and heavily armed security guards, Council members

Andreis, Vahini, Nikola and Tor, and their advisors,
including Shu and Lisa. The soiree was moved to one of
the Station's engineering workshops. Andreis assumed
the role of master of ceremonies in what was obviously
going to be a demonstration of the Iaen Gift. Tor had
played no part in the planning of this event.

An Iaen screen was the only object in the space. It was
larger than the one he had used for Eva in the hospital.
This one was almost three metres in height and four in
length. It was dark and blank when they entered.

"We need the room cleared," Vahini said.
"ArchTheocrat, if you wouldn't mind asking your guards
and advisors to wait outside."

"Of course, of course."

The order was given.

LeMay's steel blue eyes shone.

In that moment Tor wanted to confess all.

*Father, I have sinned. I have committed genocide. I
have born false witness. My entire life is now a lie.
Forgive me, please, please…*

"ArchTheocrat, we have summoned you here because
your dedication, your devotion to the Iaens is to be
rewarded," Andreis, of course, as reptilian in his charm as
LeMay was tiger in his.

"I am merely a servant of God, and His Angels."

Of course you are, Tor said silently. And a humble one
at that, aren't you.

"You of course, are familiar with this." Andreis
indicated the Iaen screen set up in the centre of the space.

"Yes, an ark that carries the Iaens' true souls."

"Well, they have a gift for us. A very special Gift,
ArchTheocrat and one we want to entrust to you to
control and administer according to your wisdom."

"I don't understand… "

"Mr President." Andreis said, with the air of a magician
introducing his assistant. His eyes, however, were hard
and brimmed with threat. He waved towards the screen.
Why would he… Christ, no.

There was a choice, of course. He could refuse, but

then the secret would be laid bare and it would be Annika and Eva who suffered most.

Unable to comprehend the horror of what he was about to do, Tor stepped forward. He glanced at Shu whose expression was impenetrable. Was this to be the assassination? A failed resurrection? An *accident*?

The screen erupted into nauseating, disconcerting, disorientating life. Now horribly familiar. Tor moved closer. The drugs in his system dulled the terror but could not dissipate it entirely.

Why was he afraid? Wasn't death preferable to the blurred, guilt-fevered misery of life right now? He drew himself up to his full height. He stared into the dizzying craziness of the Iaen screen where figures cavorted and writhed and scuttled through lightning-torn cloud and heaving oceans. He heard LeMay groan and gag. He turned briefly to see Lisa clutch at her skull and Andreis bent double. The others, Vahini and Natalia all looked ill and discomforted.

The surface of the screen bulged outwards, distorted and stretched and looked to be at breaking point; glass turned to rubber. Out stepped an Iaen humanoid. Tor dragged his gaze up to hold the thing's vacant stare. He wondered if he should kneel or –

The blow was an explosion of red, of sparks and fire. He felt something break and that feeling, that awareness of irreparable damage was profound and awful. The fracture was huge. There was pain, but it was remote somehow. It lurked at the borders of his failing consciousness. It strained to rush in and burn him alive in white hot agony the moment it was unleashed. Crimson dissolved towards blackness and he welcomed it and felt his *self* fade. There were voices here. Incomprehensible words, babbled around him as if he was trapped at the centre of a mob. He understood though. The meaning seeped through the darkness. *Need*. The Iaen imperative to expand to spread to live and be and take. Not greed, no, it was pure cold, empty need. The voices faded and quietened into silence.

At last –

Light, sudden and blinding. He fought for air, gasped and strained but nothing worked, his lungs were dead things in his chest, his throat was locked shut. The light burned and hurt.

Breath. A need to vomit, to cough and gasp. People were trying to haul him from the floor where he was comfortable and wanted to stay. He struggled but he was too weak. His head was an inferno of pain. His skull was broken. He was wounded, dying.

"Mr President. Mr President. Sir, can you hear me? Sir? Tor?"

Shu was crouched in front of him. His face a mask of concern. Lisa was at his shoulder.

Tor nodded, a small movement of his head which brought more agony. Daggers of it that speared into his temples and the back of his neck. He blinked and found that he was sitting on the floor of the workshop. The others stood around him in a loose arc, pale, shocked and frightened.

"Help me up," Tor said. Shu grabbed one arm, Lisa the other.

"Are you all right Tor?" Lisa sounded so upset and shocked, Tor could forgive the lapse in protocol. In public he was Mr President, never Tor.

He chuckled ruefully. He had been dead only a few moments ago and he was worried about manners. "I'm okay," he said. His throat was raw, his voice gruff, but he was alive. For a moment he was elated. He had crossed the deep dark river and returned.

And there was LeMay, in front of him, his eyes wide, flushed, looking as if he was in the grips of religious ecstasy. "Praise God, oh Praise Him, praise Him. Thankyou Heavenly Father for this Gift." He dropped to his knees, face heavenwards, arms raised.

The others bowed their heads, as if in prayer. Who to? Tor wondered. He had found only oblivion over there on the far side. He was bent double by a sudden wave of nausea. Shu was back immediately, his hand once more about Tor's arm. "We need to get you checked over, Mr President," he said.

"Yes, yes, good idea," Andreis said. "Get the President to the med centre."

"Of course, Mr Secretary."

"I'll come with you," Lisa said.

"Yes, yes, go!" Andreis gave them a distracted wave towards the doors.

Outside, where LeMay's and government staffers were provoked into a sudden, worried babble by Tor's obvious physical distress. Lisa shooed the small crowd away and ordered the guards to keep them back. Shu propped Tor up against the wall and demanded that one of the guards help him to get Tor into the tube runner as quickly as possible. "There's a Peace Legion ship at the dock, fully kitted out with a hospital. We need to get the President there as quickly as possible."

Blood sang through Tor's head, he was dizzy, confused. Shu wasn't talking sense. "But they want me in the Station Med –"

"Listen to me Tor," Lisa whispered in his ear. "The Station Med Centre is where you die. We have to get you on that Legion ship and away from here."

The runner arrived. Tor sank gratefully onto one of its rear seats. Shu and Lisa sat beside him. One of the guards took a front passenger seat. The runner slid into motion and hurtled through its tube, which ran outside the Station's hull. Its glass walls gave sight of the black of space, a glimpse of the vivid crescent of the moon.

"How are you going to explain my disappearance?" Tor asked Lisa. His head was beginning to clear, at last.

"That's all down to Shu. His task is to... to kill then dispose of you. Andreis, the others, don't want to know how or where. Their hands are to be kept clean. The proto is ready and waiting in the wings. It's probably already on its way to the Med Centre to pick up where you were supposed to have left off."

Where I left off. What an insubstantial, polite little sentence that was. Where I left off. Where my life ended at the hands of some assassin, probably a doctor. Now that would make sense. The murder would be clinical. Clean. No blood or brain spatter. Assassination and replacement could be carried out in a private room in the isolation wing. Out of sight. Quietly and efficiently. So discreet that there would even be presidential security guards outside the door of the room, oblivious to what was happening inside.

"The Legion won't give you away," Lisa said. "They answer to no one, although their sympathies do lean towards the colonies."

Tor closed his eyes. The Iaen voices babbled in his subconscious, fading now, but startling. Why the hell hadn't they left him dead?

No, no he needed to live. There could be no easy escape for him. Death brought no redemption, only freedom. Perhaps service in the Legion was an answer. The harsh, lonely life they led might offer some atonement.

"One day, Tor," Lisa said, as the runner entered the largest of the Station's six cavernous docking bays and came to a halt. "you'll return to us."

He gripped her hand then hugged her tight. She trembled and he realised that his attack dog was crying. He couldn't remember ever seeing Lisa cry.

"Mr President, you need to hurry." Shu was already out of the vehicle.

Two Legion medics were descending the metal stairs that led up to the main airlock. Their ship would be on the other side, clamped in place by the station's docking arm. The docking bay itself was primitive and utilitarian. A vast engineering space of tools and machinery, steel ladders and gantries. Room for three landers.

The Legionnaires were big men, one bearded and gaunt, the other tall, athletic and broad. They wore the bright yellow Legion overalls. The athletic one carried a medical emergency bag. All part of the charade, presumably.

"Thank you Shu," Tor said and shook his hand. Odd to

act out such a warm gesture to the man who had almost got him killed on Ia. "Be careful."

As Tor mounted the stairs to meet the Legionnaires, Shu called out loudly, presumably for the benefit of the guards, "You'll be fine Mr President. Peacer medics are the best there are. We will see you later in the Med Centre." It sounded overacted, a pantomime Tor didn't expect the guards to believe for a moment, but apparently they did, because no alarm was raised or weapons drawn. Or, perhaps they were in on the plot. There were no longer any certainties in Tor's world.

The medics took his arms, one each side. Tor let them. He was supposed to be unwell, still shocked from his death and resurrection.

Once at the airlock, Tor Danielson took one last look at the docking bay and at his life. He regretted being unable to say goodbye to Annika and to Eva, and it broke his heart. But perversely, it was best that he hadn't. They would still have their husband and father and, please God, no idea that he was a fake. Who knew, he might turn out to be a better man than the original.

Eva, still moved through the forest, glimpsed then lost. Tor clung to her trail, aware that he was being deceived and lured on to God knew what. His heart led him now. This was not a place where logic could prevail. The vegetation was agitated. The lower boughs of the trees writhed and twisted like snakes. The leaves rustled, yet there was no wind. The ground moved, stretched and contracted as if some giant slept beneath the surface. The air was rank with the smell of vegetation, a meld of the fresh and rain-renewed, the perfumed and the rotten.

The ground was littered with broken branches and the immense bulk of fallen trees, their trunks long engulfed and turned into near unclimbable hillocks by the verdant growth. There was light, here, where the forest cover was so dense that the silver touch of the planet's giant moons barely penetrated. Illumination provided by the vegetation itself, that pulsed through translucent stems and tree trunks and leaves that sparkled like a universe of small flames. Many of the glimpsed creatures that slunk and slithered in and out of sight glowed like the denizens of Earth's deepest oceans.

Huge invertebrates, multi-legged and segmented scuttled up and down the trees. He could feel their presence in the foliage above his head. Their consciousness small and alien, pure need and instinct. No thought, no future or past. Only *now* and whatever hunger or terror that instant held. Tor saw and felt larger things all around him, low, hulking, shuffling and growling. He was assailed by a storm of primal stimuli and emotion. Too intense for him to avoid any danger because it had become impossible to pinpoint the location of any one living thing.

Up until now he survived by avoiding threat. He survived by knowing but also accepting that at any moment it might end in the tearing of his flesh and breaking of his bones between immense jaws or the slow asphyxiation of a carnivorous plant's tendrils wrapped about his neck. Here, that moment would come unannounced, a sudden flare of violence in the white static of massed animal and plant minds. He accepted the fact. His only imperative was to follow Eva.

Hard to make progress now, although Eva seemed to have little problem with the dense undergrowth and heaving, uneven ground. All the while, she remained at the same distance from him, too far to see her clearly, close enough for him to know that it was her.

She disappeared into a stand of giant fungi dense enough to be a forest within a forest. Tor was not inclined to enter the dank darkness, so he used a fallen tree trunk as a step to clamber onto the top of the nearest of the mushrooms. Its surface was slippery and yielding. He held out his arms for balance and moved as quickly as he could over the fungal forest's canopy. A sound inveigled its way into his awareness. He was unsure when it had begun but it grew louder with every teetering, uncertain step.

A violin.

Tor didn't recognise the piece but knew that it was Eva. The melody was mournful yet beautiful. It spurred him on, gave him renewed urgency. He realised then that he was no longer fleeing the Other, he was seeking whatever lay at the heart of this forest. His pursuer was no longer important. Something waited for him and was drawing him... home? The concept was unsettling and confusing, but that was how it felt.

A huge invertebrate emerged from a crevice between the mushroom canopies ten or so metres ahead. It was a translucent, centipede-like monstrosity. Red light pulsed through its body. It reared, great pincer jaws open and lunged towards him.

Tor scrambled to his left, intending to jump from the fungus and run. He ducked beneath a low hanging branch that was festooned with twitching fleshy tendrils. Some hint of hunger boiled out of the sensory storm that filled his head, some incomprehensible version of life and awareness. It made him drop to his belly and crawl because he knew, suddenly, that he must not brush against those things, even lightly.

He heard the patter of the invertebrate's uncountable feet as it closed on him. He was almost at the mushroom's edge, slithering over its soft, treacherous skin. He wasn't going to make it. He could barely move or think.

There was a thrashing sound. Vibrations thrummed through the mushroom. He twisted around to see the centipede tangled in the tendrils he had been so careful to avoid. It struggled and twisted but it was impaled by the plant's thorns, and it was doomed. Fibrous, root-like filaments were already piercing the invertebrate's soft underbelly.

As Tor regained his feet, he experienced the centipede's terror and pain and felt a pang of sorrow for the monster. There was nothing he could do, of course. This was the way of things on Mi. This was the way of things on any planet where there was life. The moment any protoplasmic entity drew whatever constituted its first breath, the battle for survival was joined.

The music slid into his awareness again and there, standing on the far edge of the mushroom forest's canopy was Eva. When Tor regained his feet and resumed walking, so did she. Eva walked. Tor followed.

*

The woman I now know to be Katherina Molale leads me deeper into the forest. Her name had surfaced unbidden. I experience odd feelings about her. I want to catch up with her. I want to hold her and kiss her. There is deep grief as well. I have memories of making love to her. I have memories of heartbreak and then, terrible bleakness. And guilt. She should be dead. That confuses me. Worse, the feeling that I am responsible for her death, in fact, I think I killed her. This is why I need to talk to Real Tor. To understand. To feel, because all my emotions are counterfeit and such artifice will not be acceptable to those who will try me.

This place is some sort of nexus, a node in the life-network that covers Mi. The closer I get to its heart the stronger the sense of a controlling force, a mind. It's not that simple, however. That *mind* is part of something greater.

Yet, for all its importance, there is nothing here but monsters that crawl, slither and scuttle through the night shadows or cavort through the trees. My mastery of the link to those minds has grown to such an extent that I am able to avoid most of them. There have been close moments, a frantic run, pursuit. Some of the trees are dangerous too. Seemingly harmless, fragile-looking tendrils hang from some of the lower branches. They are, I sense, deadly. The problem is that the combined life forces in the forest are growing too loud for me to distinguish between background din and imminent danger.

Each step I take, requires intense concentration. The ground beneath my feet twists and swells and then shrinks. There are sudden holes and crevices. The trees split into grins and the limbs twist on themselves, this place is becoming a vortex of madness.

All the time, Katherina. She is the most maddening component of this. I cannot catch up with her. The distance between us never changes. She looks back over her shoulder. I can't see her face properly. I'm sure she calls to me but her voice is lost in the gale of other voices. I am exhausted. I can barely walk now. I want to rest. I need to rest. I stop and take a swig from my water bottle. There isn't much left. At the same time as all this, I need to watch the screen of the DNA sensor to ensure that I am still on Real Tor's trail. At least I seem to be gaining on him.

I feel an odd sense of belonging. Dangerous as it is, Mi has snagged a part of me. Perhaps it's because I do not have a home. The station on which I was born is the nearest I have to such a place, but I was never meant to stay there. I feel reluctant to leave Mi. The thought of it brings on a deep sadness and this one is mine and real. This is not a remembered grief that I can feel and analyse, but is at the same time, remote and stolen. I know that I have to leave – if I survive this forest that is – but my heart is already heavy at the prospect.

I lean against a tree. Its trunk is riven with fractures that bleed red light. The tree issues a deep groaning sound. The sound soothes me. I want to rest here. But no, I must press on.

The lights and voices creep towards insanity. The animal life here is increasingly bizarre. Two simians that meet at a single human-like head. A snake slithers through the branches, its flanks lined with tiny faces. My face. God, my face repeated over and over again.

I pass a mass of giant mushrooms that darken the forest floor to my right. I sense that I should avoid them. Another of the multi-legged creature hangs from a tree that stands on the nearer edge of the fungi, enmeshed and impregnated by thorny tendrils that hang from a branch like strands of lethal hair.

Katherina.

I remember her and break into a shambolic half-run. Closer. At last, I'm gaining on her. I can almost touch her. I reach out, my fingers brush the back of her neck. I make to embrace her and stumble instead into an empty, silent space.

No, I see her, waiting for me, once more, a handful of metres ahead. There's enough light, albeit shifting and many-hued, here for me to see that she is poorly formed. Rough-edged. Not real. I see a network of what looks like blood vessels webbed over her skin and her tunic. Strange as it is, it's also familiar, and brings a disturbing memory. I have – Tor has – seen this before.

Then, suddenly, there are ruins.

A city. Ancient. A monument to some civilisation that once held sway on this planet.

It is overgrown and partly absorbed into the forest, but its features are recognisable. I walk down a street over which green-swathed building facades curl like frozen waves. Immense openings give entrance to some of the structures. They reveal only blackness. I sense they are hiding places for terrifying beasts who wait in the dark for the unwary who seek shelter or sanctuary from the never-ending life and death conflict waged on Mi.

Ahead huge needle-slim spires pierce the forest canopy as if stretching for light. Their clean, sharp edges are softened by vines and more of those glowing flowers that sway like seaweed in ocean currents. These structures must have been spectacular when first erected. I am an insect, crude and primitive, compared to whoever built this metropolis.

Eventually the street opens out into what was once a plaza of some description. It is walled in by more of the wave-curl buildings. Trees crowd the foothills of the structures and provide the actual borders of the space. Oddly their growth does not extend to the entrance of the street I have just walked.

I notice that the trunks of these trees are webbed with the same network of vessels as Katherina Molale, who now stands beside me. She is silent and watches something that is taking place in the square.

I follow her gaze and see Real Tor. He is holding the hand of a young woman I recognise as his (our/my) daughter, Eva. Again, she is a rough imitation, again, that web of vessels nets her skin and her dress. She is leading him out across the plaza, but something is odd about the laboured way Tor walks.

He is wading, as if walking into the sea. He is sinking into the surface as if it's quicksand. I make to rush forward to help them but Katherina grabs my arm and stops me.

*

Tor lets Eva take his hand and lead him out into the plaza. The feel of her hand in his, the warmth of it, was a joy to him. It was Eva's hand, soft, slender. But he avoided looking too closely. This was a replica, poorly executed and rough-hewn, but that didn't matter. It was Eva. He was beginning to understand now and the truth was terrifying.

The surface of the space glowed dimly, but enough for Tor to see more of the veinous webbing. It gave under his feet and within a few steps he had sunk to his ankles. Eva didn't hesitate but took him further. It was soon difficult to walk and he sank deeper with each step. He felt the first stirring of panic. He could feel no solid ground underfoot. He needed to get back to the edge of the plaza.

Tor tried to turn back, but it was too late. Eva sank suddenly into the unstable ground, no, not sank, she dissolved and became part of whatever substance this was. Tor felt it give way and he plunged downwards and through its shimmering skin. It covered his face, clogged his nose, his mouth. He closed his eyes and screamed silently as he descended deeper and deeper.

*

I see it. The horror of Real Tor's disappearance as he is sucked down so quickly he barely has time to cry out. No, I can't allow this. I have to save him. I rush into the plaza. The ground is warm, fleshy but otherwise solid.

Halfway across to where Real Tor disappeared, someone grabs my hand and yanks me back. I spin about angrily to see that it's Katherina. I struggle to release my hand but her grip is supernaturally tight. She leads me back to the edge of the clearing to wait. There, I let the voices and thoughts and colours of the planet wash through my mind until it splinters my pain and brings a measure of peace.

I begin to wonder if Real Tor is still alive and what I should do if he isn't.

*

Music. The rise and fall, the sublime heartbreak and ecstasy of a lone violin that cried to him from the stage. He shook his head and looked wildly around to see that he was once again in the concert hall of the Humanity Station. There were the babbling waterfalls and the lush vegetation. There was the vast dome and the dazzling green, white and blue of the Earth. He was alone however. The only audience member, who sat in the same seat as he had done for that Sibelius Concerto more than five years ago.

The solitary figure on the stage was Eva. She wore the same dress. Her hair was long and free. Her face glowed with joy and the abandon into which she was always transported when she played.

Tor wept as he watched. He wept for the love of his daughter, but also he wept for the price paid for her life. He pushed his griefs aside to concentrate on the music. He recognised the piece. It was the one he had followed through the forest on Mi. He loved classical music, his knowledge of the genre was encyclopaedic, but this song was unfamiliar. It was also elusive. He tried to grab at a melody, at shapes and structures but there were none. It shouldn't work, and yet it did. This was not some free-form jazz endeavour, this was a thing of aching beauty. It rose and fell and weaved glowing chains about his heart and soul.

He had no idea of how much time had passed, or why, or how, he was here. Gradually though, he came to realise that he was not alone. He could see no one but he could feel them. He stood and scanned the auditorium. Something wrong. This place. He peered down at his seat. It was the correct colour and texture, but rough to the touch and webbed with a network of vessels. The ones on either side were the same. He looked up at the great arched ceiling that curved up to support the dome and saw that its surface was a veinous map.

Where had he seen this before?

The music grew louder, almost unbearably so.

Where?

Ia.

Running through the battlefield. The enemy, marines that were real-but-not-real. Approximations.

The Tal. The race he had obliterated. The price he had paid for –

He realised that the music had stopped. The stage was empty. Eva was gone. No, no, no. She was here. She had to be here. She had been playing for him. She… she wasn't here. She was back on Earth or touring the colonies. Living the life she had made for herself. The life bought with a holocaust.

And yet, the Tal were here.

They had been called here by the original inhabitants of Mi. He saw it, in his mind. He lived it. The climate collapse. The clouds of poisonous fumes vomited into the atmosphere by factories and transport, rolled across, then enclosed the sky. Tor smelled their heavy, chemical stink and coughed as they scraped the flesh from his throat and burned his lungs. The delicate, stickman-like citizens fled underground. They had stripped the planet of its resources. Its forests were blackened and dying, its seas a toxic soup rotten with dead flora and fauna.

The tunnels and shelters were a brief sanctuary. Food and water were scarce, space a commodity. Factions formed. Life dwindled to need. Survival was all. There were squabbles, fights, raids, then wars, fought in the claustrophobic warrens beneath the planet.

A few survivors reached out to the strange voices they had detected in space during the zenith of their dirty industrial and technological revolution. The Tal, benign, spirit-like had answered. The survivors had made a final request. For the Tal to save their planet and give it rebirth when the poisons had been washed away and the place was once more clean. The Tal promised that Mi would live again.

They had come, as they had to countless other worlds, as they once had to Earth. Although on that world, their messenger had been met with scepticism, arrest and a cruel public execution under a merciless Middle Eastern sun.

The Tal were Mi's id. The Tal had created the vast network of life here, taking the form of the great trees that grew in the ruins of the planet's once mighty cities. Roots were thrust down into the barely-living soil. Fibrous tendrils grew outwards, slowly spreading across the planet for thousands of years until they were joined into a vast network. The Tal had nurtured the surviving plants and animals and allowed them to claw their way back.

In the nodes, energised by the Tal's energy, life erupted and evolved quickly into the exotic and strange. The nodes were nebulae where flora and fauna, rather than stars, exploded into being. Mi lived again, cleansed and teeming, just as the Tal had promised.

Ia might have been the Tal's home world, but they had spread outwards aeons ago.

Wounds heal, Tor.

Katherina, she was speaking to him. He looked around to find himself in the ruins of the Tal city on Ia. Smoke drifted across the shattered street, Tal mind homes burned, the stink of it, the stench of burning flesh. There were bodies, uniformed, sprawled and contorted by their death agonies. Tor coughed on the awful perfumes of the place. Nothing remained intact. Everything was burned and scorched and maimed. He struggled to breathe.

Wounds heal but some are too deep to heal quickly.

Tor's skin burned and blistered. His stomach heaved and he was dropped to his knees by a sudden wave of nausea. He vomited blood. There was nothing but pain that radiated outwards from his abdomen as he suffered the indignity of radiation sickness. Fallout from the tight nuke assault, pummelled his cells and broke them down. He shivered, too weak to get back on his feet. Assailed by the death cry of the few Tal who had survived the blasts but were now dying. Their cry was a song, sent out into the universe, a lament heard by others of their kind on whatever worlds they had been invited to stay. Tor recognised it as the music the fake Eva had played in the forest and in that empty concert hall.

He lifted his head, to tell Katherina that he was sorry, but she was gone.

The burning intensified. He lifted his hand to see the flesh peel from his bones like scorched, tattered rags. He couldn't breathe. He was buried alive, suffocating. It was pitch black. He couldn't move. He needed to move. God, how he needed to breathe –

He burst upwards and clutched at the plaza's shimmering, tremulous surface. His fingers dug into the substance and he lay there, gulping in air, drained of energy and the will to move or think.

This was too much to comprehend. He was on a Tal planet and they had not snuffed him out when they could have easily done so. They had finished what the Other had started. They had torn away the final layer of protection from his own wounds. They had brought him face-to-face with what he had done.

When he looked up he saw the Other, standing on the edge of the plaza. Tor struggled to his feet and set off towards him.

*

The two stood face-to-face; the wild-looking, bearded, long-haired, primitive version and the clothed, civilised version. Although, Tor noticed that the civilised sheen was beginning to wash off. There was intense sadness in the Other's eyes. The sadness of a sacrificial lamb.

Tor waved towards the steps and sat down. The Other took his place beside him.

"I can't give you what you want," Tor said.

"I'll take what I can."

"You talked about your purpose. Were you created to stand trial?"

The Other nodded. Yes.

Tor took a breath before asking his next question. He was not sure that he wanted an answer but the question was inevitable.

"Are Annika and Eva safe?"

Are they alive? Wasn't that what he really wanted to ask.

"They are safe. They live on a station orbiting Sirius II, where I was born. To be precise, I was born on an old colony seeder permanently docked at the station. Lisa Kavanagh is there as well. She was my mentor and friend. The colonies are seeking independence from Earth. They loathe LeMay and the Council. And they don't trust the Iaens. The colonies have formed their own federation and want to rejoin the Alliance."

"Why is Annika there?"

"She knew of the deception almost from the start, that's what Lisa told me. She sensed that something was different, something wrong, about the Tor Danielson who came home to her after LeMay's visit to Humanity Station. She said, according to Lisa, that he was too perfect."

Tor laughed ruefully.

"She and Eva fled, with the help of Lisa, Shu and the Peace Legion."

"Thank God. I suppose they know the truth now."

"I don't know. Annika would have nothing to do with me."

"And Earth? The Council won't let go of the colonies easily."

"No, which is why the Federation wants to re-join the Alliance of Planets. It isn't the Council who are the threat. It's the Theocracy. LeMay has strengthened his power base. He was transformed from religious leader to messiah when he underwent death and Iaen resurrection during a vast rally in the Vatican. It was witnessed by billions, in the flesh and on vidcast. A huge segment of the military pledged their support for him. The Council was weakened. There is civil war on Earth between the Theocracy and the Council and it looks as if the Council are losing ground."

"You said that Lisa is on the Station. Is Shu there as well?"

"No. He died soon after helping our... your wife and daughter escape. Officially he took his own life. He stepped out of an airlock, no suit. Lisa doesn't believe it was suicide."

"Nor do I," Tor said.

"The Alliance are considering the membership of the Federation of Humankind Colonies. There is a price; Tor Danielson on trial. That is my purpose. No one was sure if you were alive, this is a dangerous planet. There were those who believed that you would have been driven insane by guilt. We were not sure that, even if you were alive, you would be willing to stand trial. After all, you atoned for what you did on Ia when you were in the Peace Legion. Regardless of any of those possibilities, Tor Danielson must stand trial."

"That's crazy."

The Other shook his head. "I am the sacrifice. That is why I was made. The Alliance believes that I am the real Tor Danielson. No one knows you are here on Mi, except Lisa Kavanagh and the commander of the Peace Legion unit in which you served. He was the one who brought me here. Their ship is in orbit, waiting for me. It will take me to the trial as soon as I return."

"So, that's why you need to find me, to truly

understand why I did what I did, to be convincing before the Alliance."

"Yes, but also so that I can understand who I am. I comprehend the reasons but not the emotions, not the truth of that moment when you assented to a tight nuke strike against the Tal."

"You never will."

"But, I have to."

"Who brought you here, through the forest?"

"Katherina Molale."

God it hurt to hear her name delivered in such a matter-of-fact tone.

"What did you feel?"

"Affection, strong emotions, something that might have been love."

Tor laughed, the sound odd to him because he had no idea when he last laughed. "*Might* have been? I'm sorry, that proves that you could never understand that deep part of what it is to be me, any more than I can grasp what it is to be you. Listen, Tor, there are empathic and telepathic races in the Alliance that will tear your impersonation apart. You are a good approximation, but you are you, not Tor Danielson. You have your own id, soul, call it what you will. It's untainted and whole. Mine is rotten."

The Other got to his feet. "I have no choice but to go."

"Is there a death sentence?" Tor asked.

"I don't think the Alliance have decided on a punishment yet. They consider themselves civilised, but the crime is genocide." The Other shrugged. "Perhaps they are not seeking punishment but to understand."

"Are you afraid?"

"This is my purpose. My emotions are irrelevant." There was a tremor in his voice that belied his seeming equanimity. "I admit that I've experienced things that have awakened a part of me that I did not know existed. The hurt I felt when Annika rejected me, the feeling aroused in me by Katherina. I also regret having to leave this planet. I was lonely until I arrived and came to understand it. Here, you are part of the whole." He made to go. "Goodbye Tor. I believe that you are a good man, but all humans, you, me, we're flawed. We're governed by emotions as much as by logic. Your mistake was a terrible one in every sense of the word, but it was driven by love." The Other seemed to draw himself together, as if dragging his courage about himself then set off down the wide street that ran between the wave-curled buildings of the ruined city.

"Wait, Tor, wait."

The Other stopped. Tor walked quickly to catch up with him.

"You don't have to leave."

"No, I must."

Tor took a steadying breath before continuing. "I'll be the one facing the Alliance. It's time."

"Tor, please. My purpose –"

"Come with me if you like, or stay. But you are not standing trial on my behalf. I think... I think I've been forgiven by the Tal. They showed me what I did, but also why. I understand that now. Forgiveness comes at a price. You're the good man, Tor Danielson. A better one than me. You have no crimes to answer for."

"Surely you atoned when you were a legionnaire. There's no need –"

"I need to answer for what I did. There'll be no peace for me, or justice, until I do." Tor allowed himself a rueful smile. "And your Federation of Human Colonies needs the Alliance, so there's politics in this too. That's my trade, after all, politics."

As he walked away, back along the street, Tor allowed the voices of Mi to flood into his mind, partly to guide him to the Other's lander, partly because he knew it would be the last time he heard them.

*

Yes, I am Tor Danielson. I am he but also I am what *I* am. I experience guilt as I watch Real Tor fade into the shadow and shade of the overgrown street, but I also know that he is right. The Alliance tribunal would have broken me apart easily. They would have discovered the lie concealed within, because the truth of what makes an individual who they are, belongs only to that individual and can never be replicated.

It is for me to make my own mistakes and commit my own sins. For now I am part of the teeming profundity of life that lives out each moment in that wild, desperate dance of survival. Here, on Mi, I am a part and apart. I am alone but not lonely. I may have no purpose anymore, but I am alive.

ENDS

Elsewhen Press
delivering outstanding new talents in speculative fiction

Visit the Elsewhen Press website at elsewhen.press for the latest information on all of our titles, authors and events; to read our blog; find out where to buy our books and ebooks; or to place an order.

Sign up for the Elsewhen Press InFlight Newsletter at elsewhen.press/newsletter

Also by Terry Grimwood

Terry Grimwood
INTERFERENCE

The grubby dance of politics didn't end when we left the solar system, it followed us to the stars

The god-like Iaens are infinitely more advanced than humankind, so why have they requested military assistance in a conflict they can surely win unaided?

Torstein Danielson, Secretary for Interplanetary Affairs, is on a fact-finding mission to their home planet and headed straight into the heart of a war-zone. With him, onboard the Starship *Kissinger*, is a detachment of marines for protection, an embedded pack of sycophantic journalists who are not expected to cause trouble, and reporter Katherina Molale, who most certainly will and is never afraid to dig for the truth.

Torstein wants this mission over as quickly as possible. His daughter is terminally ill, his marriage in tatters. But then the Iaens offer a gift in return for military intervention and suddenly the stakes, both for humanity as a race and for Torstein personally, are very high indeed.

ISBN: 9781911409960 (epub, kindle) / 9781911409861 (96pp paperback)

Visit bit.ly/Interference-Grimwood

THE LAST STAR

Beware god-like aliens bearing gifts

Stasis and inorganic self-repair, new spacefaring technologies for humankind, yet more gifts from its closest extra-terrestrial ally, the Iaens. There are, it seems, no limits to humanity's outward journey.

Then Lana Reed, Mission Commander of the interstellar colony seeder, *Drake*, awakes from her own stasis to discover that all but three of the vessel's other tanks are dark, their occupants suffocated, screaming yet unheard in their high-tech coffins. But the stasis tanks are not all that is dark. The sensors return no readings from outside. The external vid-feeds show only unending blackness.

There are no stars to be seen. No planet song to be heard. No galaxy cry. No echoing radio signals that proclaim life.

The *Drake* and its surviving crew are adrift and alone in a lightless, empty universe.

From Terry Grimwood, another taste of the human realpolitik alliance with the Iaen, begun in *Interference*

ISBN: 9781915304377 (epub, kindle) / 9781915304278 (144pp paperback)

Visit bit.ly/TheLastStar-Grimwood

Other Elsewhen Press titles that you might also enjoy

LOOPHOLE

IAN STEWART

Don't poke your nose down a wormhole – you never know what you'll find.

Two universes joined by a wormhole pair that forms a 'loophole', with an icemoon orbiting through the loophole, shared between two different planetary systems in the two universes.

A civilisation with uploaded minds in virtual reality served by artificial humans.

A ravening Horde of replicating machines that kill stars.

Real humans from a decrepit system of colony worlds.

A race of hyperintelligent but somewhat vague aliens.

Who will close the loophole… who will exploit it?

Ian Stewart is Emeritus Professor of Mathematics at the University of Warwick and a Fellow of the Royal Society. He has five honorary doctorates and is an honorary wizard of Unseen University. His more than 130 books include *Professor Stewart's Cabinet of Mathematical Curiosities* and the four-volume series *The Science of Discworld* with Terry Pratchett and Jack Cohen. His SF novels include the trilogy *Wheelers*, *Heaven*, and *Oracle* (with Jack Cohen), *The Living Labyrinth* and *Rock Star* (with Tim Poston), and *Jack of All Trades*. Short story collections are *Message from Earth* and *Pasts, Presents, Futures*. His *Flatland* sequel *Flatterland* has extensive fantasy elements. He has published 33 short stories in *Analog*, *Omni*, *Interzone*, and *Nature*, with 10 stories in *Nature*'s 'Futures' series. He was Guest of Honour at Novacon 29 in 1999 and Science Guest of Honour and Hugo Award Presenter at Worldcon 75 in Helsinki in 2017. He delivered the 1997 Christmas Lectures for BBC television. His awards include the Royal Society's Faraday Medal, the Gold Medal of the IMA, the Zeeman Medal, the Lewis Thomas Prize, the Euler Book Prize, the Premio Internazionale Cosmos, the Chancellor's Medal of the University of Warwick, and the Bloody Stupid Johnson Award for Innovative Uses of Mathematics.

ISBN: 9781915304506 (epub, kindle) / 97819153041407 (560pp paperback)

Visit bit.ly/Loophole-Ian-Stewart

BIRDS OF PARADISE

RUDOLF KREMERS

Humanity received a technological upgrade from long-dead aliens. But there's no such thing as a free lunch.

Humanity had somehow muddled through the horrors of the 20th century and – surprisingly – managed to survive the first half of the 21st, despite numerous nuclear accidents, flings with neo-fascism and the sudden arrival of catastrophic climate change. It was agreed that spreading our chances across two planets offered better odds than staying rooted to little old Earth. Terraforming Mars was the future!

A subsequent research expedition led to humanity's biggest discovery: an alien spaceship, camouflaged to appear like an ordinary asteroid. Although the aliens had long since gone, probably millions of years ago, their technology was still very much alive, offering access to unlimited power.

Over the next hundred years humanity blossomed, reaching out to the solar system. By 2238, Mars had been successfully terraformed, countless smaller colonies had sprung up in its wake, built on our solar system's many moons, on major asteroids and in newly built habitats and installations.

Jemm Delaney is a Xeno-Archaeologist and her 16-year old son Clint a talented hacker. Together they make a great team. When she accepts a job to retrieve an alien artifact from a derelict space station, it looks like they will become rich. But with Corps, aliens, AIs and junkies involved, nothing is ever going to proceed smoothly.

If you're a fan of Julian May, Frank Herbert or James S.A. Corey, you will love *Birds of Paradise*.

ISBN: 9781915304308 (epub, kindle) / 97819153041209 (538pp paperback)

Visit bit.ly/BirdsOfParadise-Kremers

A TRUTH BEYOND FULL

ROSIE OLIVER

Don't dig deep lest you regret what you find

Miranda, an ice and rock moon of Uranus, has been a thriving mining colony. But recently there has been a rise in fatal accidents. Kylone has an ability to extrapolate patterns behind a rock face to determine where and how to dig. When his fiancée died in another accident, he blamed himself and his ability; a wreck, no longer able to mine, he became a priest with limited duties in the locally developed Priesthood. Assigned to officiate at a hero miner's funeral, the widow asks Kylone to investigate the spate of accidents and, along with some help from an unexpected source, he starts to suspect that they may have a more sinister cause, a suspicion which puts his own life in danger.

ISBN: 9781915304582 (epub, kindle) / 9781915304483 (326pp paperback)

Visit bit.ly/ATruthBeyondFull

About Terry Grimwood

Suffolk born and proud of it, Terry Grimwood is the author of a handful of novels and novellas, including *Deadside Revolution*, the science fiction-flavoured political thriller *Bloody War*, and *Joe* which was inspired by true events. His short stories have appeared in numerous magazines and anthologies and have been gathered into three collections, *The Exaggerated Man*, *There Is A Way To Live Forever* and *Affairs of a Cardio-Vascular Nature*. Terry has also written and Directed three plays as well as co-written engineering textbooks for Pearson Educational Press. He loves music and plays harmonica, and growls songs into a microphone with The Ripsaw Blues Band. Happily semi-retired, he nonetheless continues to teach electrical installation at a further education college. He is married to Debra, the love of his life.

Printed in Great Britain
by Amazon

56657789R00078